SURVIVING THE STORM

A NOVEL

SURVIVING THE STORM

A NOVEL

I.J. MILLER

Blank Slate Press | Harrisonville, Missouri

Blank Slate Press
Harrisonville, MO 64701

For information, contact:
Blank Slate Press
www.amphoraepublishing.com
Blank Slate Press is an imprint of
Amphorae Publishing Group, LLC
www.amphoraepublishing.com

Manufactured in the United States of America
Cover Design by Kristina Blank Makansi
Cover photo: Shutterstock
Set in Adobe Caslon Pro and Gravesend Sans

Library of Congress Control Number: 2024932709
ISBN: 9781943075874

FOR KATHRYN

Every time I tried to tell you
The words seemed undercooked
So I'll have to say "I love you" with a book

SEPTEMBER 17, 1989

The first hint of trouble arrived through the speakers of Yankee's portable radio. His large frame filled the narrow, wood security shack that faced the front gate of Long Beach Bluff resort. A Rasta knit cap with stripes of red, green, gold, and black bunched his heavy dreadlocks into a thick ball on top of his head while the brim hid his eyes so no one could tell if he was napping. He sat in a wood chair, legs propped on a small stool. Yankee was forty years old, had been the security guard at Long Beach Bluff for twenty-one years, and lived just down the road in Old Hill Village. He *was* napping. But woke in a start when Peter Tosh's soulful reggae was cut off by a loud, forceful, radio voice:

"Attention! All people of Antigua! Hurricane comin. Batten down! NOW! The name Hugo and looks like the worst in a decade. Full force in three hours."

Through the shack's windowless opening, Yankee surveyed nearby Full Moon Bay. The early morning sun disappeared behind dark clouds, the wind picked up, and the normally tranquil aqua-blue water dissolved into a murky grey. He reached for the phone, pounded three digits.

Manager John answered just as he finished his morning shave. He was in his late twenties, gangly tall, from Seattle, Washington, recently promoted from assistant manager, married two years to his ultra-thin wife, Becca.

"Hugo headin this way in three hours," Yankee said. "Possibly Cat Four."

"Must have made a leeward turn. We need to start the Hurricane Emergency Plan now!"

John hung up. He tried anxiously to reach Alvin, the assistant manager, a local, dialing first his house in Old Hill Village, then his office. No answer. Alvin rarely got to work this early, and rarely spent the night in his own bed.

John rushed to the bedroom, shook Becca awake. "Hurricane's coming! Winds could be over 100. Monitor the ham radio and keep me updated. We're shutting this place down!"

Becca leaped out of bed, sprinted to the bathroom. John knew it was to brush her teeth. Becca never did anything before brushing her teeth. He grabbed the phone, jabbed the numbers for the owner's house next door. Ned picked up, about to snarl over being woken up, when John snapped, "Hugo's on his way!" Then hung up.

He exited the house, dashed down the hill, and alerted every staff person he met to start the Hurricane Emergency Plan, something rehearsed at least once a year, and was soon at full throttle. Next, he banged on the doors of the occupied resort rooms and urged a quick evacuation. The resort was only half full, since it was, in fact, hurricane season.

Taxis soon waited in line along the entrance road as guests hustled towards them with hastily packed luggage. Drivers stowed suitcases, stuffed patrons into their vehicles, swiftly accelerated off the property, towards the airport, to catch the first flight out...to anywhere.

When the last guests departed, Yankee closed the two halves of the resort entrance gate, made up of long pointy spikes, each side decorated with a half metal seashell that made one whole shell when he locked them together. Then he sprinted up the paved entrance road that led towards the offices, shops, and main dining room. To the right was the Full Moon Bay waterfront. To the left was a large swimming pool. The six waterfront staff towed Sunfish sailboats and windsurfers to shore, up to the high sand, then shackled them to the ground with a heavy tarp. With extra weight, they anchored down the one motorboat used for water skiing and fishing, then hustled to gather the beach and pool lounge chairs, piled one on top of the other, and dragged the tall stacks to the large cement warehouse behind a group of thick palm trees.

Rob-O, the waterfront director, and his girlfriend Kate, the yoga/aerobics instructor, scrambled to shutter the open beach bar and stow liquor bottles and glasses in the back room. They were in their mid-thirties. He was a bleached blond beach bum with scraggly long hair, always in a Hawaiian shirt and cargo shorts. She wore close-fitting leggings shaped against her taut, lean body like a second skin, her brown hair pulled into a tight bun.

The waiters, cooks, and dining staff raced to carry chairs and tables from the open-air dining room to the warehouse, along with the island paintings that dotted the walls. The housekeepers helped the facilities staff board up the glass on the resort room sliding doors that faced the Atlantic, as waves crashed hard and grey onto shore.

Long Beach Bluff had four two-story guest buildings on the beach, each with five rooms on the first floor and five on the second. It was a small but exclusive vacation spot. There was not enough plywood to board all the beachside sliding doors, so the staff left several open, along with the landside entrance doors, so the wind could pass through without shattering glass. They stuffed what they could—mattresses, lamps, furniture—into large closets.

Up the bluff road sat two identical, modest-sized houses. Rob-O and Kate lived in the first one, John and Becca in the second. At the top of the bluff, overlooking the ocean to the west, the bay to the east, was the grand house. Ned lived there with his wife, Twiggy. They were a childless couple, he in his late fifties, she in her forties. Ned was a short, round, pale-skinned man with puffy red cheeks from too much drinking. He inherited Long Beach Bluff from his father and had been on the property when Claudette hit ten years ago and it had taken months to refurbish the resort. Tee shirt untucked, belt still unbuckled, he burst out the front door, waddled down the hill, and snarled at any staff person he encountered to *work harder*! Twiggy—a tall, leggy blond, far too pretty for Ned, who earned her nickname from her early modeling days—raced from room to room of their house, hid artwork and lamps in closets, stowed kitchen items, put X's of masking tape along the smaller windows that dotted the walls.

"The full hit's less than an hour away!" blasted Becca's voice through the speaker of John's walkie-talkie.

But he didn't need the heads up. The wind whipped across the resort property, forced the palm trees from a sway to a bend, while the air filled with debris lifted from an open trash bin somewhere behind the buildings. There was more to do, but John advised everyone by the resort rooms, the main dining hall, and the offices to go home. He then blew an air horn so the staff at the bay knew it was time to depart. Most of the workers lived in Old Hill and needed to secure their own houses.

Ned located John at the center circle roundabout, where the entrance road circled back towards the main gate, and a large, heavy metal bell attached to a thick wood base rested on an island of grass opposite the steps up to the check-in desk.

"Why the fuck are you sending everyone home?" Ned shouted.

"They need to get out of here before they get stuck." John stood so the wind carried his words towards Ned. "We need to hunker down before Hugo hits full force!"

Ned was about to protest again when a powerful gust slammed an empty soda can into his chest and knocked him back.

John guided him up the steps, towards the open lobby.

Becca and Twiggy, arms linked, maneuvered down the hill, staggered by the barrels of wind that blasted their bodies. They were smart enough not to wear hats but pressed a hand to their heads as if to keep their hair from blowing off.

Rob-O and Kate fought their way up the entrance road, head-on into the wind, which billowed their shirts, and buffeted them as they made slow but steady progress.

They all met at the gated side door near the main kitchen and waited nervously for Yankee. Though it was midday, they watched the sky darken to an early dusk. Then Yankee burst through the trees. One hand gripped his Rasta hat flat against his head, the other proudly displayed numerous keys on a ring dwarfed by his meaty palm. "Found em."

He unlocked a metal gate, then the wood door, ducked in to pull a string that turned on a bare bulb that hung from the ceiling. Below them was a steep flight of stairs that led straight down to another door at the bottom. Yankee popped back outside. The three women and Rob-O inched inside. Ned and John hovered by the entrance.

"Do you need to get home?" John asked Yankee.

"Secured the house last night. Sent my wife, new baby, and the boys to her mother's inland place in All Saints."

John turned towards Ned, who gave no sign of inviting Yankee in.

John grabbed Yankee by the arm, pulled him inside, and said, "Close the door behind you."

All seven descended the stairs. Yankee unlocked the heavy wood door at the bottom. They entered a small concrete room. Yankee brushed past them, found a dangling string, turned on the light. Wine bottles—placed delicately, at just a slight downward incline, corks facing out, floor to ceiling, on wooden racks—surrounded them. In the center of the cement floor was a large, screened drain. All but Yankee let out a collective breath, feeling safe inside this tight, wine-filled cellar. Becca displayed a bag of snacks and fruit, with mini seltzer bottles.

Yankee said to John, "I don't have a good feelin bout this one."

An explosion pounded their ears, walls trembled, bits of concrete dropped from the ceiling, and wine bottles rattled as an H-bomb of wind and rain crashed through the resort above their heads. The light bulb went out and the three couples, along with one security guard, crouched down, and huddled so close in the pitch black they could feel the other's tremble.

"Damn," Yankee said. "I forgot the flashlight."

"Me, too," John added.

"We'll never get this place in shape for Christmas," Ned declared.

The fury continued to rage overhead, but the walls held and there was no immediate flooding.

"I hope everyone in Old Hill makes it through," John said. "I've no idea where Alvin is."

"Dude." Rob-O rewrapped the rubber band around his ponytail. "There's no way the beach bar survives."

"Anyone want a mango?" Becca asked.

Yankee accepted the handout.

"You've been quiet, Twiggy," Kate remarked.

"Just trying to wrap my head around Ned's concern for the resort while 50,000 Antiguans are at risk."

"You're so predictable," Ned said.

"No, *you're* so predictable," Twiggy retorted.

After several hours, the sudden quiet startled them as much as the storm noise had. No constant wail of wind. No pounding rain bullets. The wine bottles settled.

"Over?" Becca asked as she picked up her bag of goodies.

"The eye," Rob-O answered.

"What eye?" Kate asked.

"We're probably in the dead center right now, complete calm, but it's still around us."

Ned said, "Yankee, why don't you go up and—"

"Let's see if it stays quiet." John's voice was firm.

"I'll do it then." Ned stood.

"No." John touched his arm.

"Let him go," Twiggy said.

John held tight.

"The storm will pass soon." The group listened to the authority in Yankee's tone, the one person born on the island. "The winds may break a record. But we still have another few hours. At least."

The explosive roar of wind and rain arrived again with renewed intensity, causing an even louder vibration of wine bottles.

"Fuck this, bro'," Rob-O said. "There won't even be a waterfront."

"Just breathe, everyone." Kate's calm yoga voice resonated in the dark. "In through the nose, out through the mouth."

"Too bad we don't have a corkscrew." John ran a hand along the wine rack.

Yankee dangled his keys in the dark. "Got one right here, brudah."

John blindly selected wine from the expensive shelf. Yankee opened it. They passed the bottle and everyone partook, except Becca, not quite ready to share germs.

Several bottles later there was, indeed, a second silence, a prolonged one this time. The group staggered up the stairs, followed Yankee, each with a pressed palm against the side wall for balance in the dark.

Outside was nearly as black as the wine cellar. A stiff wind and scattered rain lingered. No electricity anywhere. The faint, hollow clang of the bell broke the bleak silence as it swayed aimlessly with the remaining gusts.

"Wait here," Yankee said.

He cautiously maneuvered towards the front desk. He knew exactly where the main patio was, centered by a flamboyant tree with blazing orange leaves. If it was still there. But he had to be careful. Debris and pieces of in-ground lamps dotted the patio. Sections of wicker gazebo walls spread across the lawn like unmarked graves. A cow could've been blown onto the property, the winds had been that strong.

He fumbled along a shelf below the front desk and fished out two flashlights. He turned one on.

"Muddah of God," Yankee gasped. He flashed the light across the open lobby. A palm tree had smashed through the women's boutique store. Brown-soaked sand had washed up to the patio. Deep puddles of water pooled everywhere.

He made his way back to the group, extended the second flashlight towards John, but Ned grabbed it. The couples zigged and zagged their way across the patio, sidestepped shaggy palm fronds, waded through ankle-deep water, glad the flamboyant made it, though it was partially stripped of leaves and had lost several branches.

"Let's go up the bluff to our houses," John offered. "We'll deal with it in the morning. Hopefully, our generator will work. The food in the storage freezer will hold until daylight."

"I'll file a claim tomorrow," Ned said. "If I can get through by phone or fax."

"Good luck with that," Rob-O smirked.

They made it to the center roundabout.

Yankee and Ned circled their lights across the property. A war zone. The dozens of palm trees that dotted the open lawns were either uprooted, snapped in half, or had lost all of their fronds and were just long, thick sticks in the ground. Shingles from building roofs spilled everywhere. The ocean had come ashore.

"This couldn't be worse," Ned groaned.

"We're alive," Twiggy countered.

"Keep the flashlight to guide you home, Yankee," John said. "Ned can lead us up the bluff. I hope your house is still standing."

"Thank you, sir." Yankee slogged down the entrance road through the heavy flooding.

As the group trekked up the bluff road, Ned zoomed his light around the property one more time, let out a loud moan when it landed on the open roof of Building One.

From down the road, they heard Yankee shout, "Muddah-fuckah!"

"What is it?" John yelled.

"Muddah-fuckah!" Yankee repeated even louder.

John grabbed the flashlight from Ned. The group followed his beam back down the road.

On the grass, just to the left, near the front gate, stood Yankee, hovered over something, as he peered towards the ground.

The group circled him. Yankee directed his light straight down and it reflected off a man's body soaked in a large puddle, face down, head pointed towards the gate. Yankee handed his flashlight to Twiggy, reached underneath the chest and turned the body over. The group gasped. Everyone recognized the assistant manager… Alvin…bulky, sturdy frame with deep, handsome lines etched along his cheeks, a head of thick, bristly, black hair, and the most remarkable blue eyes framed by his flawless dark skin, as he stared blankly back at them, his body entrenched in the mud, cold and stiff.

"He must have tried making it to the wine cellar," Becca said, her voice heavy with emotion.

"But got here too late," Kate whispered sadly.

"Debris…may have…slammed against him," Twiggy stuttered. The beam from her flashlight trailed along Alvin's body, but halted abruptly at a bloody wound across his neck. She clicked off the light.

Twiggy looked over at Ned, who quickly turned away.

John glanced at Becca, who couldn't hide her pained expression. Rob-O's gaze settled on Kate, who in turn stared back at him. "Or murda," declared Yankee.

TWELVE MONTHS
BEFORE THE STORM

JOHN & BECCA

It was early Sunday morning when John exited his house through the front door, clad in skimpy nylon running shorts and a tee shirt with a silkscreen of Full Moon Bay on the front and the words *LONG BEACH BLUFF RESORT* on the back. He stretched on the front lawn. On his feet were orange Nike running shoes, the swoosh in white. These sneakers were not for sale anywhere on the island, but he'd picked them up on his last trip to Miami.

He slow-trotted down the hill to go easy on the shin splints he had developed from training so hard the last few months. At the roundabout he kicked into gear and was off along the entrance road, headed towards the gate. He looked for Yankee in the security shack to exchange their usual waves whenever John passed by for his training runs. But the security guard was shimmying up a coconut tree—dreads hung long and shaggy past his shoulders—his arms wrapped around the trunk, bare feet flat against the tree sides as he propelled himself upwards. A guest and her young son waited in awe at how quick and agile he climbed, grabbed a coconut, slid back down. He would soon split it in half with the machete he kept in his shack and present a piece each to mother and son, his scramble a frequent performance for guests that usually earned him extra tips.

John loved all the quirks of Long Beach Bluff. Especially now that he was the manager, recently promoted after a year as assistant manager. He believed Becca was thrilled with the promotion as well.

He made a left at the gate and stuck to the right shoulder of the asphalt road so he could see the cars coming towards him, most of them with steering wheels on the right side. Though independent since 1981, Antigua was still part of the British Commonwealth.

He passed a dirt football pitch on his right that ran parallel to the beautiful stretch of bay to his left. John had first set foot on the Long Beach Bluff property when he was seven years old, during Christmas vacation. For him and his family it was love at first sight: the pristine grounds full of palm trees, perfectly manicured grass, beds of exotic, brilliantly colored flowers, resort rooms just yards from the Atlantic, hypnotized to sleep by the steady crash of waves, the beautiful, calm, clear Full Moon Bay on the other side of the bluff, perfect for water skiing, windsurfing, and sailing. They returned every Christmas, joined the many regulars who vacationed the same time every year. By age ten, he knew the names of all the housekeepers and waiters, most of them still employed at Long Beach Bluff. No locals left a job at the resort, unless they were fired.

John had studied business in college, but his dream since that first Caribbean vacation had been to settle on Antigua, at Long Beach Bluff. His parents had become good friends with Ned and Twiggy. Perhaps the offer of assistant manager was out of friendship, or payback for being such loyal customers. Ned probably thought John would quickly grow weary of the year-round position, and of the island. Very few transitioned from tourist to local: the intense heat, no TV, the worldly limitations a bigger deal when the living was permanent. News filtered in mostly through the radio, and you were lucky if phone lines were up and running. Perhaps his biggest asset was that he came from money and would not be tempted to steal.

But the recent promotion to manager was because he was good at his job: firm but fair with workers, easy manner with guests, always efficient, bringing a gentleness that buffered Ned's bluster. And he cherished everything about working at Long Beach Bluff: greeting the guests, planning the weekly meals with the head chef, supervising purchases, overseeing the groundskeeping, monitoring the staff. He was also fond of the traditions: jacket and tie at dinner, the ringing of the big bell at mealtimes, wearing all white for a set of tennis on the one ancient red clay court, the same steel band that played every Thursday night.

John had first met Becca five years ago, when her family vacationed at Christmastime. The parents hit it off immediately, both sets active with their home country clubs, the fathers taxiing off-site to Antigua's lone golf course, a scratchy eighteen holes with grass nearly impossible to keep green because of the heat and its outdated sprinkler system, the mothers from different coasts but with the same debutante upbringing. They all, joyously, approved the match. Becca had been a Fine Arts major but had little interest in art unless she was purchasing. She had envisioned a beautiful apartment in a major city, John off to work every day as a stockbroker or entrepreneur in a neat, crisp suit.

So perhaps she was disappointed with his career choice, but drew comfort from knowing that one day, with the help of their parents, they might purchase Long Beach Bluff from Ned and Twiggy—Ned always one unhealthy step from retirement—and move all the way up to the grand house.

About a mile into his run, to his left, was a long strip of empty beach with a worn twin-propeller plane buried deep in the sand. It had crashed months before John had become assistant manager and every time he ran past he scanned it, fascinated by the way the rising sands marked time. After the initial crash he could see the entire plane, down to the rubber tires used for landing. Now, one wing jutted up, the other lay buried, and the cockpit was barely visible above the sand, like a submarine taking a last peek before it submerged.

After the beach, he hit the town of Bolans. He ran through here regularly but, somehow, was still an oddity to the locals, someone to watch, even laugh at—dogs, children—men popping out of the rum shack, giving the cricket game on the radio a rest just to wave as he went by. John sometimes trained with a local runner, Marcus, who had run track on scholarship at a U.S. university. John was no match, but Marcus, the considerate training partner, stayed shoulder to shoulder, unless they ran through Bolans. Marcus would pull about ten yards ahead, no matter how much kick John called on, and then everyone seemed to be in the streets, women dropping their laundry, laughing, catcalling, shouting, "Go, Marcus!" as if the Olympic Marathon passed right through this shanty village. John waved back good-naturedly, a sheepish smile on his face, satisfied at least that they weren't yelling, "Ya losin, honky!"

As he exited Bolans, more than three miles into his run, he looked at his watch for the first time check of the day. Each summer, as part of the annual events associated with Carnival on Antigua, there was a half-marathon that started and ended in the capital city of St. John's. John was determined to make his mark in the next one and took pride in running a faster thirteen miles every time out. But his left wrist was bare, except for a perfect white-skinned watch outline against his tanned flesh.

It wasn't like him to forget.

He could continue the run for a lark.

He liked to be exact about time.

He slowed, pivoted in place, the sun now at his back, and headed home. John avoided the main road through Bolans and took a shorter way back, cut diagonally towards Long Beach Bluff by taking the beach route. It cut almost a mile off the trip and, though sand running was more strenuous, this shortcut, with his watch soon strapped securely around his wrist, would leave him fresh to begin his training run again.

John slipped quietly through the front door of his house into the foyer, where his digital watch lay in a basket on a small table. As he reached for it, he heard Becca's painful whimpers and cries from the second floor master bedroom. He bolted up the stairs. The door was half-open, but he had a clear view of his wife on all fours on the bed. Alvin, the large, muscular, newly appointed assistant manager—promoted from head waiter—was on his knees behind her. Instinctively, John retreated a step back, body hidden by the door, barely breathing, eyes glued to a sight he never could have imagined, immobilized by the intensity of Alvin's thrusts, the way he twisted a fistful of Becca's hair into his hand, the delicate arch back of his wife's neck, her strangely unfamiliar gasps and groans. After gauging the high angle of Alvin's penetration, he realized the assistant manager was deep into his wife, entering a place previously unexplored, at least by John.

"Yes, Sweet Jesus, yes," Becca moaned. "Don't stop!"

Another moment of frozen disbelief—Becca invoking Jesus was a double shock—he backed away, sprinted downstairs, grabbed his watch, out the front door, overwhelmed by the urge to run, very fast.

Of course he should've stormed into the room with the righteous anger of the cuckolded husband, put a stop to the encounter, thrown Alvin out of the house, reported him immediately to Ned to expedite the termination that would go instantly into effect, and told Becca everything he thought of her and this unbelievable violation of their marriage vows.

But how embarrassing for all three of them to be caught in such a bizarre mid-morning act. The reality of it did not compute. He shouldn't have been there. He should've been seven miles into his run.

Yankee was back inside the security shack this time and gave John his usual wave. John couldn't get himself to wave back, just kept his head down, sprinted towards the road, and made his usual left turn. The utter shame of what he had just witnessed pounded him, like the hard asphalt through his running shoes, straight up his aching shins.

He thought they had a happy marriage.

But...

"Antigua's getting boring," she had told him recently. "No place to have kids."

But Becca didn't want kids. Not yet. She wanted time to enjoy an unencumbered married life before the responsibility of child rearing dominated her days. She wanted to hold on to her thin waistline and flat tummy as long as she could before children transformed her into middle age. She had always loved Antigua, particularly Long Beach Bluff, but it was home now, not a Christmas escape. Vacation is only fun when you have a place to vacate from.

He'd tried taking her to local dance clubs, but she never got the calypso beat, her movements awkward and too fast, as if she listened to the techno music she favored in college. Had she ever seen a full moon anywhere else so white and spectacular it turned the sea into shimmering ice? She'd never adapted to the unchanging rhythm of the island. No rebirth of spring, stirrings from a brisk fall and its colorful changes, the bracing for the cold whiteness of winter. Always the inertia of blazing summer. *Soon come* meant slow, but it always got done. She still didn't understand the speech of the Antiguans, even when they avoided the local patois and spoke straight English. He had explained that she only needed to listen.

"You have your work," she had said. "I only have shopping, tanning, and swimming."

And now ass fucking. With another man.

Alvin had been with Long Beach since he was a teenage hand on the fishing boat. He was as easy with the guests as his locally famous smile but could have a hard grip with the kitchen and dining staff when needed. He knew exactly who was lazy, shifty, running a game, or stealing, and he took care of it. A big man, someone you didn't want to mess with, unmarried, but proud that he had fathered over twelve children with who knew how many women.

Once a very prestigious guest from England had her diamond necklace stolen right out of her room. It took Alvin just a day to get the word out and get it back. Long Beach would not be as successful without Alvin.

As he approached Bolans he remembered, not long ago, heading past the four resort buildings and seeing Alvin come out of an empty room. For a brief instant, Alvin seemed flustered, but then quickly fashioned his trademark grin, gave John a familiar pat on the back, and declared his usual, "Wassup, brudah mon?"

"Not much," was John's routine reply as he kept walking. He remembered thinking it unusual, but not strange, when he glanced through the separation between Buildings One and Two and saw the red of the fringed sash Becca usually wore around her bikini as she darted along the beach side of the resort rooms. She had told him she was going into St. John's for lunch.

Now, as he picked up his pace to an early sprint, he recalled the hushed whispers of the housekeepers that quieted as he got closer, the sad cocking of the head sometimes when they watched him walk away. How long had this been going on? Did everyone know but him?

No let up on his torrid pace as he exited Bolans, checked his watch: just under twenty-five minutes, a record time. His anger caused him to accelerate even more, ignoring the impact on his sore shins, the premature razor sharpness in his chest. It was a hot day, but he would not only complete his run, he would return home in a significantly shaved time so he could at least catch Alvin on the way out and confront them both.

Staying true to his training, even on the return route, he resisted the temptation to lop distance off his run by using the shortcut. He entered his front door, stumbled through the foyer, sweat dripping down his face like tears, lungs heaving, ankles swollen, staggered up the stairs. The watch showed a good ten minutes off his fastest time. The most minutes ever dropped.

But Alvin was gone. John dragged himself to the shower. Becca was already there. She stepped out of the stall, embraced him, her wet clean body against his wet dirty one, her head sideways against his chest. He remained stiff. How could she hold him? How could he hold her after she had given up perhaps the most intimate part of herself to another man?

Alvin was wide and bulky. John was tall, narrow waist, lean from running. He must feel so different from Alvin. Did the two of them even embrace? Kiss? He needed to pull away so he could look her straight in the eyes when he told her he knew what she had done. Instead, he softened to her body, to the affection he felt for her, clutched her closer.

Was she crying?

He never should've returned for his watch. If Becca knew, she would tell him it was just another of his typical anal-retentive behaviors. What a lousy fucking choice of words.

She reached for a towel, went into the bedroom. John undressed, stepped into the shower stall, turned the water on hot. He loved her. Perhaps they were already falling out of romantic love? They rarely cuddled, kissed, held hands anymore. Sex was maybe once a week. But he never stopped loving her. Didn't most couples fall out of romantic love? But was the itch supposed to come so soon?

In Antigua it came and went anytime. Single, even married guests were hungry for an adventure. Many locals spread their seed willingly and often. The non-local workers at the resort (chef, boat captain, visiting tennis pro) occasionally slipped up with guests, but most often found their adventures with the inexpensive prostitutes in town. It helped fight off the routine, the boredom. John had never cheated, never really thought about it. The first six months of their marriage they made love a lot, still experimented, occasionally found a secluded spot on the beach. Then he started running.

Did she still love him? Was she bitter he didn't take a job in finance? Can someone actually love one person and have anal sex with another?

He started keeping closer tabs on Alvin, beeped him on the walkie at odd times with forced questions John hoped weren't too obvious. Maybe it was better if he was obvious. Maybe if they thought he was suspicious they would stop.

He stopped running. Completely. Which meant he was around on Sundays.

Their lives didn't change. Except there was a weight that hung over him, sagged his shoulders, slowed his walk, as he wondered if the pair somehow still found time to engage, or if the Becca he knew wasn't the real Becca. Or if perhaps he never knew his wife at all?

Alvin was his same jovial self at work, still looking to shoot the shit during their free time, to talk about old school reggae versus today's dancehall style. John couldn't understand how Alvin could be the same after what he'd done. But Alvin didn't know John knew so why should things be different?

He decided that if he caught them one more time, he would confront her. If she wanted to leave him, she could. He didn't want to lose her, but he wasn't sure he wanted to fight for her either, after what she had done. If she wanted to stay married, but wanted to leave Antigua, he would let her go. He would confront Alvin, too, tell him he could kiss his plum job at Long Beach Bluff goodbye. John didn't think he had to worry about Alvin initiating more encounters with Becca. There were plenty of others he could shack up with under far less scrutiny than John applied now.

Not too long after his training run misstep, Becca threw John a splendid birthday party. She was all-smiles, often sliding her arm through his as she stood by his side. Though surrounded by friends—Ned, Twiggy, Rob-O, Kate, Alvin, Yankee—John smiled like he would towards the guests, an appearance that looked the same, but lacked a deeper warmth.

The next day he drove into St. John's. He'd heard of a place on Front Street that was supposed to be clean, upscale. He paid his money to an older woman and was told to make his choice. It didn't matter what she looked like, so he chose the woman who sat in the seat closest to him. She said her name was Raven. She grabbed his hand and led him upstairs. In the small, dark bedroom she sat on the bed but he sat on the one chair. He wasn't sure why he was here. Perhaps, like his wife, he wanted a secret.

"What's your name?" Raven asked.

"John."

She giggled, revealed white, straight teeth. She must have thought he made it up. Raven surely wasn't her real name.

"Wouldn't you be more comfortable sitting here?" She patted a spot next to her on the bed.

"I want to ask you something." John slid forward in his chair. "Let's say I was handsomer, maybe had a more muscular body. Let's say I massaged you from head to toe, paying particular attention to your feet. I make you so relaxed you practically forget where we are. Let's say I'm a great kisser and spend hours just kissing and licking you," she moaned her approval, "taking time to discover the parts of your body that make you really hot. Then let's say I'm erect the whole time and you really don't have to do anything but lie back and let me make love to you for as long as you want until you're completely satisfied."

"Come here now, lover, you're making me all wet just talking about it."

"No," John said, sharply, startling her. "I want the truth. It's just you and me inside the room now and the thing I'll appreciate most from you is your honesty."

She cocked her head, looked at him quizzically.

"Just tell me the plain, simple truth," he continued. "If I somehow could make all this come true, is there any possible way that I could reach you, that I could arouse any genuine emotion in you, for me?" She still didn't answer. "The truth now. I won't be mad."

She shook her head no.

"Not that you aren't handsome," Raven said. "And I'm sure you can do all that you say. But it just can't happen in this room, no matter how great your moves are, not with someone who just paid. I could never turn my head around that much, here."

John stood up. "It's sweet of you to be so honest and I appreciate it." He took out a one-hundred-dollar bill and laid it on the bed by the spot she had patted. He walked towards the door.

"Let me ask you," she said, stopping him. "Suppose you found me very sexy, and I did all the same things to you right now, here in this room. Could I reach you in some way?"

He lowered his eyes to the floor. "I don't think so." And left.

It was a Sunday morning, one month after John had caught Becca with Alvin, when she slept beside him as he lay in bed, eyes wide open. He listened to the waves crash against the rocks below the house on the Atlantic side. Then he listened even more closely, trying to determine if he could actually hear the water lap to shore at Full Moon Bay on the other side of the bluff. Could he? Or did he imagine he could?

John acknowledged that life down here had a numbing effect, that maybe it was just too routine to feel anything deeply. Though he was a very hard worker, he had lost some of the ambition he had in college. No urge to change anything around the house, to cook new foods, to take up an instrument, to indulge in a new hobby. He had no vision of himself in the future aside from growing old at Long Beach Bluff as Ned had, as so many others were doing. The thing was, he was not unhappy. In a book he read in college, the writer wrote that the key to happiness was having something to do, something to look forward to, and love in your life. John thought he had all three. He liked waking up with Becca, sharing this house with her, having her on his arm when they greeted new arrivals. He would like to have children with her.

But was she happy?

Well, that was something she had to decide for herself. He couldn't change what she did or didn't want. She would never leave him for Alvin. But John would not tolerate her happiness including someone else in her life. If he caught them again, for sure it would be over. The good thing about not much changing around here was that things rarely got worse.

John propped up on one elbow, leaned forward, kissed her on the cheek.

She stirred softly and whispered, "Good morning, sweetie."

"I'm going for a run." And he was soon out the front door, watch strapped securely around his wrist.

ROB-O & KATE

The first rays of dawn split the window blinds, smacked Rob-O in the eyes, and startled him awake. He sat up, still clad in last night's Hawaiian shirt. The messy bedroom spun before him as he reached a hand to his temple: a hangover the size of a small country. He stood, legs shaky, knocked over an empty rum bottle on the floor, which spun loudly under his night table. He staggered to the bathroom, opened the door.

"What the fuck?" said the naked blond girl who sat on his toilet.

"Who the hell are you?" Rob-O asked.

"Last night you called me *unforgettable.*"

A short while later, showered and shaved, fresh Hawaiian shirt and cargo shorts, he headed down the bluff road towards the waterfront. The naked blond girl was long gone. He *vaguely surmised* that she must be a guest, here with a bunch of girlfriends, the group who closed down the bar last night.

A busy morning: Fix the compressor in the scuba shack and fill the empty tanks. Give a windsurfing lesson to an elderly guest who had told him this was on his bucket list. Wax the water skis. Restock the bar.

He liked busy. It kept him out of trouble. Hopefully John or Ned didn't see the girl slip out the back door of his house halfway up the bluff. He liked his job, too.

In the afternoon, he worked behind the bar, freed up staff to serve drinks to those either pool side left, or bay side right. In an open area, surrounded by palm treed shade, the new girl, Kate, led an aerobics class. She had on tight leggings, which revealed shapely calves and thighs. She wore her usual baggy sweatshirt cut down to short sleeves. Rob-O didn't understand why a sweatshirt in this heat. With unending vitality, she encouraged the ladies and two men to follow her lead as she performed various dance moves to the beat of heavy bass rock music.

After the class, just the eight middle-aged ladies found seats at tables, still in open air, but under the beach bar roof. Rob-O approached to take orders and make friends. Kate helped serve, along with Lucky, a teenager with short braids from Old Hill Village who was carving out a future for himself at Long Beach Bluff. Rob-O discovered the group was from Long Island, NY, and this vacation was their annual Bridge Club Outing.

"I can't stop *shvitzing*," said a plump woman in a one-piece bathing suit as she wiped herself down with a hand towel.

Rob-O wondered if that was some kind of drink she wanted, but there was no follow up on her part.

After he served drinks, Rob-O stood in the center of a large painted circle on the main patio and banged a metal tray with a long wooden spoon. Everyone turned towards him.

"Ladies and…" he surveyed the room. "Ladies, welcome to Long Beach Bluff's Beach Bar. You're fortunate to be here at this hour because it's time for Rob-O's Famous Crab Races."

The ladies perked up, all eyes on him.

Lucky made a grand entrance out to the circle, carried another tray, but this one covered with a metal lid, as if he was about to present a giant turkey. Rob-O moved aside, and Lucky placed the tray in the center of the circle and stepped away. With a flourish, Rob-O bent down, lifted the lid. The ladies rose as one to see five land crabs, all with numbers taped to their backs. Before the crabs could scurry away, Rob-O topped the tray with the lid.

The ladies dropped down.

"We numbered the crabs 1-5. You predict which crab will exit the circle first. If your crab wins the race, you double your money. Lucky will take your bets and give you a ticket with the appropriate number. Minimum bet $10 U.S."

The women dug excitedly into their purses or beach bags, produced cash normally reserved for tipping.

Rob-O had correctly predicted that the bridge club ladies would be the gambling sort. He was at the bar when Lucky brought him the money.

"Heavy on numbers 1, 3, and 5."

Rob-O nodded. A small white handkerchief was in his hand. He crouched down to the almost floor level shelf behind the bar and reached for a brown bottle, the word *chloroform* on the label. Still ducked low, he held the bottle then looked at the handkerchief, lost in thought while he decided.

Kate stood nearby. She cleared her throat. Shook her head.

"I can't afford the 1, 3, or 5 winning," he whispered.

"You got a great gig here. Why risk it by grifting old ladies from Long Island?"

"The money's good."

"So is your job."

She left with a tray of rum punches.

Who was this new girl? Here only a couple of weeks and already formed an opinion. He was still undecided. If he placed crabs 1, 3, and 5 off the tray, into the center of the circle with a chloroformed handkerchief it would guarantee 2 or 4 would win.

He stowed the handkerchief on a shelf, went back to the circle, ran the race legit. Number 5 won and he lost forty bucks overall, but several ladies were ecstatic, and shrieked with delight, as if this was the highlight of their vacation.

He gave Kate a dirty look.

She smiled back.

She had a beautiful smile.

He said, "Dude, you're gonna have to make this up by—"

"Shouldn't I be *dudette?*"

"*Dude* is an omni-neutral term."

"You mean gender neutral?"

"How about accompanying me tonight to hear the Steel Band All-Stars at Shirley Heights?"

"Okay."

"That was very decisive," said Rob-O.

"One of us has to be."

"Are you saying I'm indecisive?"

"Don't get me wrong. I think you're amazing. Great water-skier, instructor, windsurfer, diver. You seem able to fix anything."

"I didn't think you noticed."

"But when it comes to making decisions, like what to order for the bar, or maybe wearing a different outfit, or whether to drug your crabs, you do seem a tad, well more than a tad, *unsure.*"

"Firstly, I *choose* to wear the same outfit every day. Secondly, I have powers of observation as well and I noticed that you like everything perfect. I see how you make sure all the liquor bottles face labels out when we close up each night. The chairs precisely tucked in against the tables. Yoga mats washed every day, always spaced the same distance apart as they hang out to dry. That bun of yours never with a hair out of place."

Kate laughed. Her laugh was pretty, too.

"Two imperfect patrons of paradise," she offered. "What can I say?"

"That I should pick you up at eight."

"Okay."

"Where do you live?"

"A small flat in St. John's."

"Stay. I'll make sure they serve you dinner."

"I don't have a change of clothes."

"It's a live band at an outdoor venue."

"Still."

"I don't care if you stink. I made a concrete decision to ask you. The least you can do is be less than perfect."

"Okay, but I'm buying. Help make up for the crab beating you took this afternoon."

"I'm actually looking forward to this, Kate."

"I'm impressed you know my name."

It was her first live steel band. The outdoor bar was a mix of tourists and locals. Each member of the band stood behind steel drums ranging in height and banged the calypso beat in perfect unison. All the aerobics had paid off, or maybe it was her natural rhythm, but Rob-O couldn't take his eyes off her as they danced. She quickly caught on to the island style: feet forward and back, hips swaying side to side to the sound of drumsticks hitting steel. She added an occasional samba flourish—forward, back, a dramatic spin, as her ponytail flew, then faced right back at him without a missed step.

"I think I'm in love," Rob-O said.

"I never felt so far away from the States and being a kindergarten teacher as I do right now."

"Kindergarten?"

He grabbed her right hand in his left, put his right hand on her left hip. She put her left hand on his right shoulder. They continued to move in perfect unison.

"Teaching wasn't so bad," Kate said, as she breathed evenly, totally in shape. "But after ten years I figured I better make a move or this might be it."

"So you landed here?"

"The water, the beach, the sun...the music!"

She did a sudden dip and wiggle and he managed to stay with her.

"And you?" she asked.

"When I got out of college, I couldn't decide what to do."

"What a surprise."

"Buddy asked me to be first mate on his sailboat for an extended Caribbean cruise. Awesome time. Didn't wear clothes onboard for a month. Then we docked here. They needed a waterski instructor. I stayed on. A few years later the waterfront director got fired for skimming off the top. The rest is history."

"So, it's by default."

"I prefer karma."

After more dancing and a handful of Red Stripe beers (he only allowed her to buy the first round; he made decent money and lived rent free), he walked her up to the nearby Heights, quiet and peaceful, a high cliff with a glorious view of the sea below and the bright stars above.

"I never want to go home," she said, eyes glazed from the beauty surrounding her.

"I am home."

He kissed her. Her lips were soft and tender. He wasn't drunk. He wanted to be clear because something about Kate felt different. She was her own person. The intensity she put into her classes was truly impressive. She didn't put up with his shit. All of it made her that much more attractive.

As they kissed, his hand moved over the sweatshirt, from her belly, up towards her breasts. She grabbed his wrists in a firm wrestling move.

"Too fast?" he asked.

For the first time she appeared unsure.

"You're a great kisser. And I'm sure a wonderful lover. But...I'm a late bloomer."

"A virgin?"

"Hardly." She paused, still awkward. She pulled her loose sweatshirt tight against her chest and both nipples were barely outlined through the material, without any real bulge of breasts. Her eyes lowered to the ground. "A late bloomer who never really blossomed."

"I don't give a shit."

"When I know you well enough to believe it, I think it'll be really good."

They walked to his car. He drove her into town and parked in front of her two-story building. They both looked straight ahead. She waited for him to do something.

"Are you giving up on me?" she asked.

"Not sure what to do next."

She kissed him on the cheek. "Thanks for understanding."

"Thanks for not making fun of my indecisiveness."

They laughed. She exited the car.

On the way back to the resort, two things surprised Rob-O: still sober, still interested.

There was something about being around her electric energy during the night that he wanted to match. It would not happen if he was drunk. He usually liked getting drunk with the many women he slept with, mostly hooking up at other resorts or bars with single ladies or bored housewives on their own looking for the *complete* Caribbean vacation experience.

When they were drunk, it was less likely they noticed he had a small penis.

He worried in high school. Got over it. The insecurity returned about a year ago after he got John to buy the resort's first VCR, monitor, and portable video camera, large and bulky, big enough to snap a VHS tape inside to record. He used it as a teaching tool for water skiers, and sometimes made short vacation videos for the guests to earn extra money. He hoped to get an underwater camera soon for the scuba divers. When alone, he also occasionally watched porn: used video copies with unmarked covers, made from originals, picked up at a store in St. John's in the midst of a blossoming video rental business.

And every guy had a bigger penis than he did!

But he was sure that the reason he never settled down, or even stayed with someone long enough to call her *girlfriend*, was simply because he was a very free spirit.

For date number two—he never usually went on *dates*—Rob-O invited Kate to dinner at his house. She wore a beautiful, flowered sundress, with thin straps over the shoulders. He could see that, for sure, she was flat-chested, but it did not affect his belief that she had an awesome body.

He wore a different Hawaiian shirt and pair of cargo shorts than what he had on at the waterfront.

She looked him up and down. "I guess I don't have to peek into your closet to know what's there."

"Why mess with what works? Comfortable. Stylish. Backs up my Surfer Dude image."

"I suspect there's more to the image."

"Are you here to find out?"

"I'm here because you offered a home cooked meal."

"That you shall have."

He led her to the balcony overlooking the ocean. A small round table was set for two. A bottle of white wine, procured on the DL from the new head waiter, was already open and breathing.

"Wow," Kate said, as she looked out at the ocean. "I didn't know the view from here was so spectacular. They must think you're special."

"I share the place during Christmas and New Year's with the visiting tennis pro."

"Beats the resort rooms."

"Ned and Twiggy's house has a view of the ocean and bay, with balconies facing both."

"Can't have it all."

"I never wanted it all. Just a decent level of comfort."

"This is more than decent."

"Now that you're here."

He poured the wine. They clinked their glasses.

"To my first home cooked meal on Antigua," toasted Kate.

Rob-O served Antiguan Ducana and Salt Fish, with a side of spinach. He had to bribe the head chef for the recipe by trading a scuba lesson. The Ducana was a local sweet dish of shredded sweet potato with coconut flakes and raisins, boiled into a crispy packet inside aluminum foil. The Salt Fish was sliced cod, fried with tomato sauce, vinegar, with green, yellow, and red peppers.

Kate took the first bite of her fish. Stopped. Kept the morsels in her mouth. Breathed in deeply through the nose. Then swallowed. Then sighed. "I think every woman must have her weakness—a foot rub, a back scratch, a brilliant dancer, a—"

"Big penis."

She laughed, head back, as her eyes squinted, the sound from her belly. "Any man who cooks for me. Goes straight to the heart."

Dessert was local Antiguan Black pineapple. Small in size. Exploded with sweetness.

"Best pineapple I've ever had," Kate said, as she wiped golden juice from her mouth with a cloth napkin.

When they finished, she did not help him clean up, though she would later, just grabbed him by the hand and led him to bed.

They kissed deeply, in harmony, undressed each other at the same time. Rob-O didn't hesitate to touch, kiss, caress her bare chest and nipples. Her head went back and she moaned her approval. He was soon erect enough to enter, but politely asked, "You on birth control?"

"Diaphragm."

He nodded, then looked at her, hesitated.

"Already in."

"You knew I'd be that easy?"

"Oh, yeah!"

He entered her, delighted with her moistness, or was that from the diaphragm lube? When sober, he usually worried more that he wasn't able to penetrate deep enough, but as he rolled her right nipple gently between his thumb and index finger, and heard her soft moans, he became less concerned. She didn't seem to care about his size. Maybe he was bigger than usual because he wasn't drunk? How could he be self-conscious if she wasn't?

Their lovemaking created a neat symmetry of melding bodies that moved the same way, with the same intent, as they did on the dance floor. Sweat mixed, along with saliva, as they kissed. Bed springs coiled and uncoiled. Deep grunts and shrills of pleasure. Rapid and grand. But the beat wasn't the repetitive sound of Caribbean steel drums that build to a finale, rather the rising climax of a rock power ballad, all instruments in synch, crashing towards the same crescendo.

Her moans increased, rapid, loud, more frequent as she arched her hips to meet his thrusts. He looked into her eyes. She closed them.

Then he could no longer control himself and wailed like some 80s band frontman (Brett Michaels? Jon Bon Jovi? Van Halen? Axl Rose?), "You're such a hot, sweet fuck!"

She topped his fierceness with a final scream that overrode his.

He collapsed on her. Then rolled off. They stared at the ceiling as their chests heaved in unison.

Finally, still out of breath, he whispered, "You faked it, didn't you?"

A pause, then a deep breath, as if she was about to speak, about to refute. Then she settled into the bed with a soft sigh.

"I tried so hard when I got to college not to let my booblessness define my existence. I started swimming competitively, just daring someone to comment on my *streamlined* figure. Competing gave me confidence. I had boyfriends. But either I was too pissed at my body to make the warm connection I needed, or my body wasn't satisfied marking me forever as a middle-schooler. Either way there's a certain discord." She picked up her head and looked right at him. "I loved every minute of it, Rob-O. You gave me glorious attention. I wanted you to be just as happy."

Tears budded in her eyes.

He pulled her to him. She rested her head on his chest.

"It's cool," he whispered. "I loved it. The scream at the end just got a little too *Debbie Does Dallas*. I want to let you know that you don't have to pretend. Really. I know sometimes I'm just not big enough to satisfy women completely."

"What are you talking about?"

He looked down at his flaccid penis.

"It's not your penis. Your penis is nice. I'm very attracted to you. I enjoy sex with you. I like how you kiss, how you touch me, how you make love. I just can't get off."

"You mean like *never*?"

"Never."

"Even alone?"

"Even alone. I've tried everything from tantric breathing to a vibrator. It's not you. It's my road that always leads to a dead end." She wiped away her tears. "I can go home now if you want."

"I don't want you to leave. I want you to stay. As long as you want."

"What do you mean?"

"We can pick up your stuff and move it here. I love being with you."

"But what about the non-orgasms?"

"Oh, that," he said, with the confident tone he used when one of the waterfront staff fretted because the ski boat engine wouldn't start. "That won't be a problem."

The first night she moved in, Rob-O had her lie on her stomach, in his double bed, naked. He warmed coconut oil in a bowl with a candle. Kate looked at him and said, "I might like this better than a home cooked meal."

When the oil was warm enough, he whispered, "Don't speak."

She obliged.

He started with her shoulders and back, gently. The warm oil allowed his hands to glide over her flesh in a soothing rhythm. She moaned.

He moved to her thighs, calves, then feet.

He turned her over and worked her nipples, belly, inner thighs. A hard squeeze produced a deep bass sound. A light caress evolved into a soprano. She was his instrument and he played her.

Then he kissed her.

Then he entered her with his finger, and she let out a soft cry.

He massaged her there, inspired her wetness, circles, then up and down. He curled his finger deep inside her, touched an uncharted place, and her breathing turned rapid. He worked that spot, over and over, tried to build towards a climax, as her body squirmed. But she could not plateau. And his hand cramped.

He flopped onto his back.

A long silence, until she said, "We really can't make a big deal about this. I've enjoyed everything so far. Sex can still be great without an orgasm."

"Since when?"

"Maybe more for women."

"Women don't want to come?"

"Sometimes they don't need to."

"But never?"

Another silence. Both on their backs. He realized she lived with him now. He could not be obsessed with fixing this problem.

"Okay," he told her. "Every day of the week we just do it. Normally. Like that first night. But I get one day a week. Let's make it Wednesdays. Hump Day."

"Of course."

"When I give it the old college try."

"Where did you graduate from?"

"I never graduated."

The next Wednesday, he used rope from the waterfront and lightly tied her wrists to the headboard, her ankles to the bedposts.

"Call me Master or Sir," he told her. "But only speak when given permission."

"Yes, Sir."

"Did I give you permission?"

She lightly bit her lip and shook her head, tried hard not to laugh.

He lifted her ass and gave it a slight spank.

"You can speak."

"Thank you, Master."

He made love to her. He talked the whole time. Gave her permission to respond.

"You love Master's large penis, don't you?"

"Oh yes, Master."

"No one's ever done it to you so big like this before."

"No, Sir."

"You're mine completely."

"Yes, Sir."

"My penis owns you."

"Oh, yes."

"Oh yes, what?"

He spanked her ass again. This time with a firm hand as the slap echoed off her tight buns.

"Oh, yes, Master!"

He increased his vigor, breath escaped in bursts, while he roughly played with her nipples. She responded, enjoyed the attention.

Then he arched as deep as he could, ordered, "Touch yourself. Now!"

She complied.

And he tried to go even faster. And she tried to rub herself faster. But they spun on a wheel, together, round and round, with no path towards an exit.

Until he finally collapsed into a sweaty heap. She looked at him as if she wanted to speak. "You don't need my permission anymore."

"Do you want to come?" she asked. "I could lick you, or you could—"

"If you don't come, I don't, at least on Wednesdays."

She slipped her arms out of the loose ropes and hugged him tight. He hugged her back. "Fair enough."

The following Wednesday, during their break after lunch, they put on swimsuits and went for a dip in the bay, but not before he had her insert her diaphragm. On the shore were several older female tourists who bartered with a local who sold beaded necklaces and bracelets. Rob-O and Kate drifted about thirty yards out, the water just above his waist, chest high for her. They stood, faced the beach, she in front of him. Rob-O waved to the ladies. They smiled and waved back.

He caressed her under the water; his hand slipped into the front of her bikini bottom. He pressed his quickly forming mini-bulge against her buttocks, wondered if she noticed. He waved again. All six women waved back. "They're watching us," Rob-O said. "They know what we're doing."

"Hardly."

Rob-O reached his hand down and pulled his penis out, erect, but still underwater. He lowered her bikini bottom and slowly entered her from behind.

"Do they know now?"

"I. Hope. Not."

They made love, her waist underwater, her body between his and the beach. They both smiled, waved. The women seemed to watch. Did they know?

"Rob-O, I don't want to lose my job."

"They can't help watching. They're turned on. Can't you see? They like watching you receive pleasure."

"It feels good."

"And naughty."

"Very naughty."

"More like wicked, letting me penetrate you from behind, out in the open, with everyone watching."

She closed her eyes. She seemed to concentrate on meeting every one of his slow, rhythmic thrusts with her own subtle hip swing back.

"It's wonderful," she said. "I want you to come in me."

"No. It's Wednesday. Not unless you do."

She opened her eyes. "It feels really good. And I like being watched. Don't you? My great big stud boy. Doing it out here in broad daylight just so some ladies will have a vacation they'll never forget."

"Stop, Kate. You know I won't unless you do."

"You can't help it. I'm so tight. So slutty. So needy. You're so *big*! Come in me. With that great big horse cock. Now!"

He did, as he lost all inhibition, unable to resist her dirty talk, some last thrusts, a bit of a yelp. The women had to know.

But when Rob-O and Kate waded to shore, after discreetly washing themselves and adjusting bathing suits back to a proper fit, the ladies just smiled warmly, and waved one more time.

A full moon was out on the following Wednesday. Rob-O and Kate strolled hand in hand, along the ocean beach side, past the resort room buildings, towards the bluff. Moonlight shimmered along the water, so bright you could play a set of tennis.

"Where are we going?" Kate asked.

"A secret spot no one knows about. We'll be hidden. If we can't orgasm, at least we'll experience nature's full glory."

"I knew you were a romantic."

"Dudette!"

Their laughter came easy now. They fit as well as an old pair of sneakers.

Once they got to the rocks below the bluff—their house, John's house, and the grand house above them—Rob-O looked back to see if anyone on the beach could see them. Most of the guests were at the large patio off the main building, on the other side of the resort rooms. A DJ was set up under the flamboyant tree for a night of dancing.

Rob-O ducked down. Kate followed his lead. They weaved their way around the bend, past tall black rocks that jutted out of the ground, until they came to an open sandy area—hidden from the resort rooms, and the beach behind them, invisible even out at sea because of the rocks at the shoreline—where Rob-O was prepared to work his magic one more time.

Except there were two figures already lying on the sandy area.

Rob-O and Kate immediately dropped behind a rock, then raised their heads a bit so their eyes peered over:

Twiggy and Alvin.

They scrunched down again. Kate looked at Rob-O, her wide eyes and head nod clearly communicating that maybe his spot wasn't as secret as he thought. Or maybe the look was *Oh, shit, I can't believe the assistant manager is doing the owner's wife?*

Kate silently laughed and Rob-O loosened up. Then he signaled with his head that they should go back. Kate shook her head. She peeked up again, then Rob-O did, and they watched.

Twiggy and Alvin were completely naked, their clothes to the side in two separate piles. Twiggy had her eyes closed, legs spread wide, Alvin's face buried between her thighs as he crouched up on his knees, while his head moved in the same rhythm as his tongue. Twiggy pressed her lips together, tightly, seemingly so she wouldn't scream. Alvin's penis, fully erect, extended from his waist all the way to the sand.

Rob-O gave one more head signal to go. But Kate silently giggled her *no*.

She watched. Rob-O watched, but mostly he glanced at Kate, her eyes glued to the action below them. Then, to his enormous surprise, Kate reached a hand into her shorts and rubbed.

The scene of Twiggy trying desperately to contain her passion, but to no avail, and Alvin grunting with messy pleasure and effort, as he feasted with his mouth and tongue on his divine meal, aroused them both. But Rob-O was sure that all Kate did was stare at Alvin's magnificent erection.

Kate's breathing quickened as Alvin's efforts doubled. Rob-O froze from the potential of simultaneous climaxes by Twiggy...and Kate.

But though Kate seemed oh-so-close, she faltered, again, tried doubling her efforts, but then the tide rolled in full force, flooded this square of sand, washed over Twiggy and Alvin, circled around Rob-O and Kate's legs.

They didn't need a silent signal. Rob-O and Kate took off back towards the main beach and ducked immediately between Buildings Three and Four, the ones closest to the bluff, hidden in the dark. They looked back. Twiggy now wore a damp skirt and blouse. She walked calmly along the shoreline, away from them, as if on a moonlit stroll. When she got to the end of Building One, she veered towards the main buildings. Alvin, in khaki shorts and a white shirt, stepped from behind a rock, scurried towards the nearest beach exit, which was between Buildings Three and Four. Not wanting to give themselves away, Rob-O grabbed Kate and kissed her deeply. Alvin dashed by. His body and clothes dripped with sudsy water.

"Pardon. Have a nice evenin."

When he was well gone, and probably trotted discreetly across the lawn and out towards the gate, Rob-O and Kate burst into loud laughter, then covered their mouths in case guests were in the rooms nearby.

"That was amazing," Kate whispered.

Rob-O nodded. He didn't want to say anything else and risk losing some of the magic of what almost seemed to happen.

The very next Wednesday, Rob-O led Kate again to his not-so-secret spot.

"Are you sure we won't run into Twiggy and Alvin?" Kate asked.

"I can guarantee it."

"Guarantee it?" she repeated with curiosity. "Well what about the tide?"

"We're here earlier this week."

It was a darker night, but they took one more look back to make sure the beach was empty before they ducked behind the rocks. They weaved their way past more rocks and finally made it to the sandy area.

To Kate's great surprise, Alvin was there waiting for them. Alone.

Aghast, she looked at Rob-O. He smiled.

"Go with the flow," he murmured.

All three of them undressed, Kate more slowly than the other two. Once naked, Rob-O looked at Kate then at Alvin's penis to see where she looked, but he couldn't tell.

The two men laid her gently on the sand. Kate seemed nervous. Rob-O kissed her gently and said, "Remember, it's Wednesday."

They caressed her all over, two pairs of hands, both rough from manual labor. Rob-O so familiar. Alvin so different.

She closed her eyes.

Alvin rubbed her feet. Rob-O massaged her nipples.

Then Rob-O kissed her while Alvin put his mouth between her legs.

Kate opened her eyes; her body stiffened. He was too much of a stranger.

She looked at Rob-O. With his eyes he implored her to give it more time.

"Okay. All right." Then with a cocky nod, she ordered, "Kiss each other."

"What?" Rob-O exclaimed.

Alvin laughed. "Who knew you such a kinky bitch?"

He grabbed Rob-O's face and kissed him deeply on the mouth.

Rob-O struggled to pull away, but then side-glanced Kate who already had a finger between her legs that rubbed furiously. He stayed.

Kate clearly enjoyed being in the background, a fly on the wall, watching.

But to Rob-O's surprise, she wasn't looking at Alvin's penis, but stared at them as they kissed over and over.

She rubbed herself with increased vigor as the two men made out, right there, for her pleasure.

It began as a slow rumble. Then started to soar, to rise, as if a giant hammer landed on the base of a carnival game and shot the heavy block up closer and closer to ringing the bell. She massaged up and back, side to side—as the men kissed—rubbed until her mouth flew open. Then the bell tolled, and out came a sound that was unearthly in its delight, epic in its proportion.

It was a scream that seemed to harken frustrated nights alone in bed during high school, confused dates in college, and all the past Wednesdays since moving in with Rob-O.

The two men stopped kissing and just stared, amazed at her sounds, how her body twisted in the sand, as if a lifetime of pleasure had arrived all at once to climax with the scream, "I love you, Rob-O!"

The tide finally rolled in, but it was the least of their problems. The voice of Ned thundered down from his balcony, unable to see them, but he clearly understood that something was amiss when he shouted, "WHAT THE FUCK IS GOING ON DOWN THERE?"

They grabbed their clothes, scooted to dry land, stayed hidden behind some rocks in case Ned produced a high-powered flashlight.

Rob-O said to Kate, "I love you, too."
Then to Alvin, "Not a word, bro'. Not a fucking word!"

TWIGGY & NED

Twiggy and Ned slept on a king size bed in the master bedroom of the large grand house on top of the bluff. Multiple bedrooms occupied the second floor, each with a private bathroom. The master bathroom had a floor to ceiling glass window that faced out to sea. Unless someone on a boat had a telescope, the view was safe. The downstairs had a living room large enough to have a full resort of guests up for a party, which happened every Christmas. The kitchen was almost as big as the one off the main dining room. However, even though Twiggy was rail thin and tucked near her edge of the bed, with Ned balled up on the other side, the mattress still wasn't big enough.

If there was a lighthouse on the bluff instead of their house, the foghorn for ships wouldn't be as loud as the deep bellows that rose from the cavern of Ned's round, pink, potbelly, up through his throat, out of his nose and mouth, and shattered the night's quiet with blast after blast of world-class snore.

Twiggy's battles to buffer the sound happened either half-awake or half-asleep. She was never sure. Only sure she never slept. Ned had the nerve to open his eyes at this very moment to complain about her tossing and turning.

"Twiggy, it's like every night you wrestle with a demon and lose."

"The demon is you, Ned. I'm going to record it one day so you know what I'm up against."

"Go back to sleep."

"Who sleeps?"

"Exactly. You tug the covers, flip me sometimes. Bury yourself under pillows then throw them in my direction. Don't think I don't know you kick me occasionally."

She kicked him every night.

He added: "And I know why you stay so thin. All that scooting around the bed in a circle like you're covered with bugs."

He likely had no idea that sometimes she curled in a ball at the bottom of the bed, her legs bunched tight against her chest, so she could avoid a direct line of fire from the snorts that exploded from his bulbous nose, or the choking that machine-gunned out the pie-hole he called a mouth.

He probably didn't know that when they first turned in at night in their air-conditioned bedroom, tried laying side by side in traditional husband and wife manner, he slept higher on the pillow, the top of his head closer to the headboard, and pulled the sheet and thin blanket up to his chin, which made it cover her mouth, so she had to snatch it back down to breathe, and that even as he slept they continued their tug of war as he unconsciously jerked the covers up, she back down, until she flipped him as he so accurately described.

Ned added, just as he turned away from her and drifted back into his own personal dreamland, which pissed her off even more, "And why...do you always pull the top sheet out from the bottom of the bed?...Can't you leave it in on my side?...My feet get cold.... *Zzzzzzzzzzzz, honk, honk, honk!*"

She staggered into the living room, plopped herself on the couch, tried to close her eyes and doze. But they popped open. There, on top of a bookshelf, stood her lone ice skating trophy, won at age fifteen when she had displayed competitive promise. Ned insisted they keep the trophy there so when they had their lavish parties, he could show her off.

No one would guess their battles. Whenever they were down at the resort, whenever they were near a guest or someone from the staff, she was a loyal, obedient wife, always at Ned's side, supporting him as best she could. She *was* the golden girl for all to see.

But that, too, was becoming more difficult.

Fashion Week, New York City, 1969, her first big modeling gig. She was all legs, had been since puberty, why she looked so good twirling on the ice in her teens. Ned was in the audience, tracked her down after the show.

"I'm putting on an event at the Caribbean resort I own, Antigua Fashion Week. Would you be interested in a free seven days by the ocean, along with a stipend?"

She hesitated, though new to modeling she had already received numerous too-good-to-be-true offers.

"I'll need two of your friends," he added. "Fly you all down First Class. You can share the same room."

That seemed safer. She recruited two other models and made the trip.

Ned was better looking back then—no potbelly, less pink, more hair on his head, though he was still short.

From the first day, he took care of her. Picked them up personally at the airport, pointed out the sights. Twiggy thought her two friends were prettier, but he seemed to focus more on her. She liked the extra care. Her parents had never divorced, but it was like being raised by a single mom, her father had been so absent.

Ned never made a pass, but invited her to the gazebo each night, after her modeling show, or after that night's entertainment, for caviar, and another expensive bottle of wine or Dom Perignon. Far more platonic attention than a Midwest girl like her was used to. On the last night he invited her to his house to see the view. He sensed her hesitation and touched her hand, the first time he made intimate contact.

"I like you, Twiggy. I won't do anything you don't want."

She wasn't sure what she wanted. She was a little drunk. She felt she owed him something. It was the last night. He had been nothing but gracious. He made her feel secure.

It was six weeks later when she called him long distance to tell him she was pregnant. If he asked her if she was sure it was his, she would've hung up and dealt with it on her own. But he said, "Come back to Antigua. Let's make a family together."

The tendency for most hyperactive designers and wealthy clients she had been introduced to was to assume that someone in her business had loose morals, or at least a very modern view of the world. But she had not left her conservative outlook at home. She was pro-choice, but always knew what her choice would be. And she did not feel completely capable, nor did she think she could afford (she might have to stop working) to raise a child on her own.

How bad could life be living on the beach at an exclusive, *five-star* Caribbean resort?

They married. She miscarried. He did not hold it against her. They kept trying. She stayed on as the stylish hostess, as much a part of the resort as the noble palm trees, the elegant waterfront, and the gourmet meals.

She could not get pregnant again.

Was that why he became less interested in her?

Or was it because he woke up each day with the same person and it finally kicked in that she was simply a woman, with her own quirks, unattractiveness, natural humanness that was not anything like the glamour of her made-up, dressed-up self?

Five, six, seven years into their marriage his attention in bed gradually diminished. And she found it difficult to sleep. And he was no help.

She tried desperately to hang on, to keep them together as a couple and not repeat her mother's marriage, to find her niche at Long Beach Bluff. She shaped her role: greet the guests upon arrival, at the dining hall, and during evening events. Engage them. Make them feel as if they vacationed at a relaxing second home.

She was good at it. She was great at it. Ned was awkward with the guests. And he knew it.

But having a niche didn't mean having a life. She wanted to be more than his trophy. The day she started the Old Hill Village Fund, in 1979, was one of her happiest moments. Most of the resort workers lived in this village down the road. Guests often donated. She applied for grants. Convinced Ned to divert some profits her way. Twiggy used the fund for anything essential. If the potholes in the road got bad and the government wouldn't help, the fund did its part to pave the road. If the children needed schoolbooks, she bought them through the fund. A medical emergency someone couldn't afford, she was there. Like the time an old man went conch diving after drinking rum and got the bends. The fund paid to have him airlifted to the closest hyperbaric chamber in Puerto Rico. And when a bad storm hit, the Old Hill Village Fund was always available to help rebuild.

She became a shoulder to lean on for the resort's female staff when treated unfairly, harassed, or when they needed time off because a baby was coming or a child was sick at home and the mom couldn't afford to lose her job. Twiggy listened, closely, saw them each as individuals. She sometimes believed that most of the locals were invisible to Ned.

She would hound Ned if she had to, picked her battles, so he knew she was serious when she asked for something. The worker got her pregnancy leave. A male boss received a warning. She was the *yin* to Ned's *yang*, providing a balance whenever she could, though since John came on board, the staff seemed better settled.

But the requests made to Ned were always painful. Not because she had trouble asking, but because he didn't take her seriously, as if he didn't want to see her as more than the long-legged woman on his mantle.

He didn't like when she drove, insisted it was too dangerous for her with the steering wheel on the right while driving on the left. After all this time, did he think she couldn't figure it out? It took a month after he had a new electronic alarm system installed in the grand house for him to show her how to turn it on or off, as if she was too lame to push buttons correctly. She had no access to their bank accounts. Always had to ask him for money, even when she paid bills or bought something at the store.

Maybe he behaved this way because he was just so fucking insecure that he had to make sure he controlled everything, including her?

Sex boiled down to the use of her hand or mouth. Did he really think that she wanted no attention at all? And when even that became difficult—he took too long, sometimes unable to come—all that remained was the consistent skirmish of sleeping in the same bed and their *private* bickering.

And he wouldn't let her sleep in one of the guest bedrooms either, perhaps afraid word would get out with housekeeping, then to the rest of the staff, maybe to the guests that paradise didn't extend up the hill, to the top of the bluff, to the grand house. Ned had too much ego.

The loyalty and devotion she needed from him while he courted her had turned rigid and sometimes cruel. She often thought about having an affair. As payback? Or simply because she ached so much for pleasure? Or both?

She didn't know, as a man in his fifties, if he even had an interest in sex, or orgasms, or simply couldn't get hard anymore, or just found his release somewhere else. She didn't care.

But she was in her forties.

She had witnessed her mother's pain over many years because of her father's cheating. The arguments. The promises that it wouldn't happen again. Then the excruciating discovery of a hotel credit card bill, or the scent of perfume on a shirt, or the ridiculous reasons why her dad came home late. Or didn't come home at all. If her mother found the courage to confront him, it usually meant a massive argument, or his disappearance for an extended time, which finally settled into a marriage where husband and wife lived apart.

Twiggy remembered when, at age sixteen—as she sat quietly at the dinner table, her father absent, his setting untouched, while her mother picked at her food without appetite—her mom said, "No matter how lonely or needy a person is, that person owes it to the other spouse, the person you married and who married you back, not to have sex with someone else. It's completely selfish and unfair to exchange a moment's pleasure for a lifetime of hurt inflicted on someone who enriches your life, whose presence is part of why you have a life."

Twiggy remembered being curious why she didn't mention *love*, or at least having someone who enriched your life with *love*. She understood it meant that even if there was no love, or if it had been there, but had vanished, you still owed fidelity to the person you married.

Yes, Twiggy had found a niche, developed it into a life, as her mother had as the parent of an only child who loved her back and gave her some of the attention and comfort her mother needed, but where could Twiggy get the attention *she* needed, where she could find a life that included, *for her*, the smallest bit of pleasure?

Her mother had never met Alvin.

With yoga-like intensity she focused hard on *not* watching him, on not giving him attention that was any different from what she offered any other staff member. But it was difficult not to notice his thick calves when he wore shorts to the beach, the rippled muscles of his forearms, the beautiful smile full of white teeth, his penetrating blue eyes set against his handsome, dark face.

One late morning she had a cup of tea at a corner table of the empty dining room. She watched a delivery man push a large box across the patio on a wooden dolly with wheels. Alvin supervised. It was a new oven for the kitchen. But when the delivery man got to the six stairs up to the dining room, which led to the kitchen, he could not lift the box off the dolly by himself. Alvin ripped off his shirt, joined in, did a deep knee bend, and the large unit was off the ground, up the steps, placed back on the dolly. She was nearly breathless with the sight of his washboard stomach, a bulging, well-formed, distinct eight pack of beautiful muscles.

Did he notice her stare? Why did he have to take his shirt off?

When he came back out from the kitchen, he looked over at her, his smile extra wide as he said, "Everything in place, Missus."

She couldn't speak. Just nodded. And she hustled to her small office beyond where the accountant did his work.

She vowed not to slip up again.

But just days later she returned from a walk to Old Hill Village, and as she passed through the gate she heard the heavy beat of music from Kate's aerobics class. It surprised her that Yankee wasn't at his post, but then she looked towards the beach to see him and his wife (who worked in the laundry room) and a shirtless Alvin joining in. Twiggy liked this new girl, Kate, who had recently approached her and asked if the staff could participate in classes if they had free time. She thought it a splendid idea and said, "Don't mention it to Ned. Keep it going as long as he doesn't find out."

She forced her legs to hustle away, before Yankee or Alvin looked over, along the entrance road, up the bluff, a hurried slam of the front door behind her as she stopped in the living room to catch her breath. She was out of breath not because she was out of shape, but because of the thoughts that raced through her head.

Ned was in St. John's meeting with the Minister of Tourism whose palm Ned greased regularly to have him look the other way because certain positions at the resort were not held by locals, when the law dictated they should be.

It was an out-of-body experience as she hustled to the second floor, grabbed the telescope on the Atlantic side balcony that Ned used to observe the stars and nearby planets, dragged it to the large window that overlooked the bay side, pulled the curtains together but left enough space for the lens to peer through, and planted herself behind the eyepiece, found her destination, zoomed in, focused on her target. The telescope was strong enough so that she could, or at least imagined she could, see the sweat drip down Alvin's hard body—as he writhed with rhythmic dances moves—from his shoulders, on a curve around perfectly hard pecs, then in, out, and around, like a pinball at play around bumpers, all along those beautiful abs.

Her breathlessness continued. She had an urge to slip a finger under her dress and find the perfect spot that would provide beautiful harmony to the song she heard in her head. But she felt dirty enough already. This secret way of looking at such a glorious man—and the now unfamiliar wetness it produced—thrilled her enough.

She promised herself no eye contact as she came down for breakfast early the next morning—Ned still in the shower— though tempted to leave behind her new turquoise wrap and dine in her bathing suit. But once she saw Alvin greet guests, she unconsciously evolved into her old runway walk, shoulders back, core tight, as arms swung, one leg straight out in front of the other, in sandals with small heels that arched her calves, as she floated across the patio.

Maybe it was the walk, maybe he had gleaned her reaction to him when he removed his shirt the other day, or maybe he somehow could tell a telescope had found him and knew who was on the viewing end of it. *No, impossible.* She knew his reputation around the island, but he was smart enough always to keep it strictly business between them, the owner's wife, who held control over a job he could not afford to lose.

Except today his eyes bored into her, somehow took in her entire body without a glance down her tall frame, and said, "Looking lovely today, Madam."

She couldn't remember the last time Ned looked at her the way Alvin did—perhaps Ned never had—as if he wanted her for breakfast.

She didn't want to feel old just because she was in her forties.

Alvin was even bolder that night at dinner as she dined with Ned, the dining room at modest capacity, she in a long pale green dress, Ned in his jacket and tie, which was slightly askew. The waiters all wore the same black pants and blue floral shirts. But Alvin worked the room in his crisp black suit, shoulders pad-less but naturally broad and well-shaped, white shirt, black tie. When she finished her lobster, she placed her napkin on the plate. Alvin approached and said, "Let me take that for you."

No one noticed. Ned certainly didn't notice. But she did. Alvin's hand delicately, and discreetly, stroked the inside of her wrist before lifting the plate.

It had been so long since she had been *touched*. The graze of his fingertips along her flesh sent jolts up her arm.

It was a week later, Ned was in Miami at a hotel convention, when Twiggy invited Alvin to the grand house to repair a light fixture.

She had barely talked to him, even looked at him since he had touched her wrist. The electrician would be the person to take care of this business. But she was too frazzled to come up with anything more subtle. Subtlcty had disappeared between them for over a week now.

She knew he would understand the invitation. She knew he would come up the road in a way and at a time when no one saw him enter (or eventually leave) her house.

She started with the pretense of leading him to the kitchen to the broken light fixture, but he did not follow. Just stood there, smile ablaze, his expression now completely unabashed as his eyes reflected to her how beautiful he thought she was.

She suspected that all of it, the touch, the look, the smile, was well-practiced. And that she was just another woman in a long line.

But that didn't stop her approach, her deep kiss on his mouth, the touch of their tongues. She felt his desire for her, his need to caress her. And it thrilled. To be wanted. To be hungered for. To be lusted after.

She slipped her hands under the back of his shirt, traced her fingers up along the curves of his strong spine, circled around so she could cup his pecs, which made her palms feel petite as she grasped at the fullness of this man.

He picked her up and carried her to bed. She insisted towards a guest room. He removed her dress, bra, and panties with a hurried lust, yet careful not to tear anything. He attacked her nipples with his mouth, sucked, licked, cupped a breast in each hand, at once like a giant beast and a tender lover.

They were both naked and his large member announced itself as an additional presence in the room. This, too, thrilled her. He buried his face between her legs, his tongue thick, yet light, as it penetrated her, licked, found all her spots, as if he loved her. She knew he did not, but it felt like love when a man was so tender yet forceful, so attentive, down there.

Twiggy was about to come when he pulled away, abruptly, and she let out a disappointed groan. He kept her needy, as he lined himself over her, prepared for penetration.

"No," she whispered as she turned her head to the side.

"What?" He froze.

"Probably something I should've discussed first, but how does one talk about such things? Especially before they happen."

"Afraid I'll hurt you?"

She looked down at his extraordinary manhood and considered that possibility. But she shook her head.

"Call it old-fashioned. Call it the ridiculous notion of a middle-aged woman. Call it illogical. Call it trying to honor someone I love who passed on. But, somehow, if we don't go all the way, it'll feel less like cheating. Something I'm not really cut out for."

Alvin seemed to understand. There was no more discussion. They kissed again. Then he went back to the play between her legs, finished her with his mouth, inspired an animal intensity that she could stifle in sound (so as not to alert the entire resort), but not with feeling, as she thrashed under him and poured her wetness into his mouth which he devoured like a starving man at a banquet.

Then he got up on his knees, straddled her body, executed a few quick strokes of his vast member—that was so large and close to her face it seemed to eclipse the light from the window—and ejaculated onto her belly, the warm trails against her flesh added to the post-orgasmic surge. His final act, one that marked her completely as his.

They lay side by side.

She cleaned her belly with wads of tissues from the nightstand, then said, "If Ned finds out he'll kill us both."

Alvin nuzzled her neck with soft lips, nibbled at her earlobe, then kissed her gently on the mouth as she moaned into his ear.

"I'm very discreet," he whispered.

He washed up in the guest bathroom, put back on his briefs, tee shirt and shorts. She watched his deep muscled glutes as he exited the room.

Then she fell into the deepest, most blissful sleep she had experienced since becoming a married woman.

SEPTEMBER 18, 1989

John, Becca, Rob-O, Kate, Twiggy, Ned, and Yankee stood around Alvin's body during the dark morning hours. They did not want to leave him in the puddled grass to rot, at the mercy of stray dogs, insects, a wild boar, but it might be a crime scene. John found a tarp to cover him. Yankee volunteered to stay with Alvin. He settled into the security shack, which the wind had toppled, but it was still intact and only needed to be lifted upright and repositioned. The surrounding palm trees had shielded the structure from the full brunt of Hugo's wind as it whipped off Full Moon Bay. The rest of the Long Beach Bluff residents went to bed, exhausted but wired. A sense of their acute human vulnerability to the forces of nature, and whatever other forces were out there, had fully announced itself during the last twenty-four hours.

Long Beach Bluff was one of the few places that had electricity the morning after Hurricane Hugo hit Antigua, thanks to the gasoline powered generator Ned had installed five years ago that John got going just as dawn arrived. Then John made his way to the security shack to relieve Yankee, who drove the resort's utility truck into St. John's to the main police station. It was a grim ride.

He had to veer off road several times because of flooding and debris, disheartened by the ongoing sight of torn up beaches and broken palm trees, but he made it.

St. John's was also a mess, as if someone had swung a giant wrecking ball through the streets, into buildings, and turned the city into a mass of garbage and crumbling concrete. Residents wandered in stunned silence, tried to clear roads, discard trash. Yankee parked blocks from the station, unable to drive further because of flooding from the nearby port. He walked straight into the one-story police building and found Antigua's lone homicide detective sitting in his office, water pooled at his feet, shoes soaked. This man— short, plump, grey hair on the sides, a highway of baldness down the middle, in a cheap navy suit with white shirt and red tie—also doubled as the person in charge of security for the Prime Minister's residence, and for the two weeks of Carnival every August.

Detective Reggie.

No one was sure if Reggie was his first or last name. Most thought he simply preferred one name only, like the footballers, Pelé or Maradona.

He stood to greet Yankee. "Wah u ah say, Youngblood? Know it's not good news. Don't know when they'll be any again on the island."

"Alvin died last night."

"Wooo, a shame. He always make me laugh. Storm get him?"

"Not sure. Throat cut. That's why I'm here."

Detective Reggie was all Reggie for a moment, as he slipped deeper into patois. "Did di gyalis life finally ketch up tuh him?"

"Dat rude boy did love di gyalis."

Ned toured the resort property. Debris was everywhere and included broken wooden signs that used to read *DON'T TOUCH,*

BOAT RENTAL, NO EXIT. Half the roof was gone from Building One. The tennis court net had collapsed, blown against the buckled green fence, the red clay court by the bay side of the bluff gusted bare by the wind. The plywooded rooms held. Ned assigned staff, those who had shown up for work, to mop floors and dry the interior of rooms left open at both ends. They kept the overhead fans running. Workers covered the roof of Building One with several large tarps tied down to wooden stakes in the ground.

The water on the Atlantic side had come all the way on shore, passed through the separation of each building, trailed onto the main lawns, down the road to meet the water at the bay. By morning, the ocean had receded backwards, leaving a swamp of wet sand. The beach between the back of the resort rooms and the ocean was practically gone, a muddy mess. Tons of sand would need to be trucked in. The beach bar roof down by the bay had collapsed, but the boats remained safe.

Twiggy walked into Old Hill Village to assess the damage. No one had died. Several houses had collapsed. Roof shingles were everywhere. The village was on a hillside above the water, so flooding wasn't a big issue, but many fallen trees had caused damage to structures and cars. Groups of men, women, children moved from home to home to clear away the chaos—remnants of old automobiles blown off front lawns, bricks, wooden beams, branches, twisted bicycles, tires, odd pieces of furniture, kitchen stuff—all carried to an empty lot at the far end of the village.

The townspeople were grateful Twiggy was there. She made a list of the most pressing needs: food and water supply, return of electricity, removal of the garbage and debris from the lot, secure shelter for those in need.

Rob-O and Kate tended to the waterfront with Lucky, who, graciously, arrived early to work. Wind driven coconuts had smashed into the mirror behind the bar, shards of glass everywhere. The broken roof needed to be removed from the patio, the dock needed repair, and sand needed to be pushed back to the beach.

Becca sat quietly in her room, fought off a dark feeling of despair. She pondered bringing a sandwich down to the security shack for John.

Ned knew it could be months before they opened again, unsure when the regular electricity would come back, phone service would return, and the airport would open.

They would all learn that as bad as Hugo had been blitzing through Antigua, it could have been worse. Places like Guadeloupe and the U.S. Virgin Islands had way more damage. Death had also been lenient, taking only two other lives—aside from Alvin—while over twenty had passed in the U.S. when the violence of Hugo swept the Carolinas.

Later that morning, all seven of the Long Beach Bluff survivors encircled Reggie as he stood over Alvin's body, photographed it and the surrounding area. Reggie had gotten an ambulance and driver to bring him to the resort. Yankee had returned in the truck.

"Gate open or closed during the storm?" Reggie asked.

"Locked," Yankee replied.

"This how you found him?"

"He was in this spot, but face down," Twiggy answered. "We turned him over to see who it was."

Reggie nodded, deep in thought, then donned rubber gloves and touched Alvin's face and body, looked closer at the cut throat and dried blood that surrounded it. He pressed his bare wrist against Alvin's forehead, nodded again.

Then he stood up, studied a trail of wet sand that started at the waterfront bar and ended near Alvin's body.

Reggie gave the order for the driver to bag Alvin—Yankee helped—then carefully removed his gloves. The group looked on, eager for insight.

"I'm goin to Alvin's house to see what there," Reggie said.

"Murder or accident?" Ned asked.

"Too early to tell what caused the cut at the throat and whether he died in this spot, or dumped here, or dragged by the wind." He re-examined the trail of sand from the beach bar. "Or washed up from the bay."

Rob-O shuffled his feet and looked out towards the water.

"The medical examiner will do an autopsy." Reggie rotated his gaze to each person who stood around him. "You all together in the wine cellar during the entire storm?"

Group nod.

"He may not have died during the storm," Reggie concluded.

Becca let out a soft moan.

"What do you mean?" Twiggy asked.

"When the last time any of you saw him alive?"

"Morning before yesterday," John offered. "We talked about preparing if Hugo took a bad turn. He went home for lunch and didn't come back. I assumed to lock down his house in case the storm hit."

"Anyone else?" Reggie asked, as he studied the eyes this time.

Ned remained silent but met Reggie's stare with a hard gaze. All three women looked down at the ground.

"Why do you think it might've happened before the storm?" Twiggy asked.

"Rigor mortis has passed, which means he coulda died up to thirty-six hours ago. The body's already at ambient temperature."

Reggie nodded towards the driver. Yankee helped the man carry the bagged body to the back of the ambulance, slide it inside past the open doors.

Becca hurried up the road to her house. John rushed after her.

Rob-O and Kate advanced towards the waterfront to resume cleaning.

Reggie perused the surrounding area once again, closer to the bay this time. He abruptly crouched down, put on another pair of rubber gloves, picked up the top half of a clean broken rum bottle, avoided the jagged lower edges by grasping the neck, inspected it closely, then bagged it.

He looked up, saw Rob-O watching him.

Twiggy told herself to do something. To move her feet. To pay her last respects to Alvin at the ambulance. To say goodbye to Reggie. To ask a question. Any question. Ned just stared at her, shook his head, then ambled up the road, towards his office, just to the right of the front desk, to check if a miracle had occurred and the phone lines were back up, and to find and review the resort's Disaster Insurance Policy. Twiggy replayed a scene in her mind, over and over, something that happened two days ago at lunchtime, after Ned had gone into St. John's for a meeting to discuss the government's plans if disaster hit…

Alvin didn't go home for lunch. Met her at the grand house. Frenzied rush to the guest room. More intensity than usual with the storm pending. Heard something (or thought she heard): kitchen cabinet? footsteps? water poured? toilet flushed? Not sure. Alvin's mouth pressed deeply between her legs as she shuddered against him. But he stopped too. She motioned for him to hide in the closet. Threw on her pants and tank, rushed downstairs. No one there. Patio door open. The wind? She closed the door. Twiggy scooted upstairs, whispered that Alvin should leave quickly, through the lower back door that exited to the side of the house. He did.

Twenty minutes after Alvin left her room, she had walked down to the main building and froze when she saw Ned there. She searched his face for any hint of discovery. Her hands trembled so wildly she tucked one in each pants pocket. But it was the usual pink-cheeked blankness. He said to her, as if he answered a silent query, "Meeting cancelled."

And now, as Reggie walked towards the ambulance, Twiggy pondered saying something to him, privately, about her relationship with Alvin and what happened two days....No she couldn't say anything....Unless she knew more.

Her hesitation lasted. Reggie got into the passenger side of the ambulance, and it departed through the gate, made a right turn towards Old Hill Village.

Alvin's house was small, on the right side of the road, the cement painted pink with white trim. The ambulance parked in front. The driver waited inside. Reggie got out. Alvin's door was wide open. Reggie entered the house. Clearly a disturbance had occurred—table overturned, broken dishes on the floor—but it was unclear whether it was a personal struggle, or just the storm. Either way, Alvin had not secured his residence.

Reggie took photos, then put on a fresh pair of rubber gloves. He looked carefully at the silverware on the floor, examined sharp-edged knives for any sign of blood. In the bedroom, the back windows were blown out, and the mattress was whisked off the bed, up against the wall. Everything was soaked with water.

A small wooden nightstand with one drawer had toppled over. Reggie lifted it upright, opened the drawer. He found wet postcards from women in the States thanking Alvin for a great vacation, envelopes with nude photos, a few letters written in local patois that expressed deep love and desire. The last letter, at the bottom of the pile, had been creased into a neat square. Reggie's careful unfolding revealed a creamed colored paper with a full seashell crest at center top. Long Beach Bluff stationery. It had the quick scrawl of someone in a hurry.

Stay away from her! Or there will be consequences!!

The letter had no date or signature. Reggie put the drawer contents into a plastic bag, sealed it, brought it outside with him.

Alvin's elderly neighbor waited by the ambulance. She wore a light blue dress, her grey hair wrapped tightly in a red scarf, black slippers on her feet, wrinkly arms wrapped around herself, face marked with deep lines of perpetual worry.

"Hello, Juanita," Reggie said.

"How go?"

"Not good. Alvin passed. He's in the ambulance."

Juanita released a sad sigh, looked at the ambulance, crossed herself. "In the wrong place when Hugo hit?'

"Definitely the wrong place," Reggie said. "But not sure it's the storm."

"All survived in Old Hill. The other villages nearby as well."

"Y'always have your fingers on the pulse, Aunty."

"That a polite way sayin I'm old?"

They laughed together. Reggie saw her crooked teeth and spaces where teeth had been.

"Keep your eyes and ears open and let me know if you hear somethin."

"Will do, boss."

Reggie opened the passenger side door of the ambulance, then turned towards her. "When the last time you saw Alvin?"

"Haven't seen him since before the storm," Juanita replied. "Him don't come home much."

"Know where he usually spend the night?"

A wry laugh. All teeth and space again.

"That be like me knowin all the places where the wind blow."

NINE MONTHS
BEFORE THE STORM

BECCA & JOHN

Everything about her affair with Alvin, if you could call it that, went against her truest nature. Of all her friends and family, she was the least self-destructive. She followed a careful diet that avoided red meats. She worked out every day. Her hygiene was impeccable. She avoided negative people. Yes, she had a phobia about germs, but she hardly got sick, constantly wiped down kitchen surfaces, had the bed sheets changed every two days (she would've preferred every day, but she didn't want to hear it from John), never took a local taxi, trimmed her nose hairs daily, plucked her eyebrows, strived each morning to present nothing less than a pristine appearance.

So why did she let Alvin have anal sex with her?

Three months ago, they thought John had found out, or at least was suspicious. He stopped running. He checked up on them more than usual. Alvin told her they had to chill.

Then John started training again. Gave back their time. Rushed. Frenetic. Sweaty. Mind-blowing.

And very dirty.

She always rushed to the shower. He didn't use a condom. He never offered. She never asked. She had heard about AIDS.

She did not want a divorce. She believed she loved John. She wanted more. More of what? Antigua was always beautiful, but always the same. Would life in San Francisco or Manhattan be better?

Yes. Maybe.

So much more to do. So many more friends to have. Which meant less time to be so obsessive about the things that bothered her. When it got cold, they could vacation in the Caribbean.

But what exactly would she do no matter where she lived?

She had pondered this question each month of college senior year until she barely graduated. She had picked Fine Arts as a major because she loved paintings and sculpture. But she struggled with the hard stuff in class and her grades were poor. She tried part time jobs—waitress, librarian—to have the satisfaction of making her own money, to feel useful—but it was tedious. Just like exam time, at the end of each semester, when she became enveloped in a womb of doom. The therapists her mother made her see were of no help. She eschewed medication, not liking the side effects. She finished college with a diploma but no life.

How was anything a life when there wasn't one significant job she could do? She was out of the habit of working. Not that she ever had the habit. But school was work. To her.

John was life.

Being at the resort was life.

But *whose* life?

The early part of their marriage showed so much promise, the sense of possibilities lifting her out of her doldrums. But it didn't last.

What kind of life could it be if there wasn't one productive thing she did each day for anyone else but herself, while her husband was consumed with perfecting all the moving parts that would make Long Beach Bluff a flawless island within the island?

She admired Twiggy for her charity work and her role with the female staff. But that wasn't her. Becca could only be who she was.

Who was she?

John's wife. The resort manager's wife. Private house. Dressed for gourmet dinners each night. Tempted by various watersport lessons with Rob-O, but too chicken to try anything but a short sail as a waterfront staff steered while she laid back, big sunglasses over her eyes, and explored new vantage points to deepen her tan.

How could she expect more?

John was kind, thoughtful, and despite his preoccupation with running and running this place, he never forgot he had a wife.

She believed he loved her. He said he loved her. Despite her parents' devotion, she couldn't remember either telling the other they loved each other. Even birthday cards had the *love exchange* pre-printed on the inside page, the only personalization a penned signature.

She wanted kids. But she didn't want to be the type of wife who had kids to fix something. She needed to be sure she had a life before bringing another person into their world. She needed to be sure she could handle the difficult parts of raising a child with John's full support.

These doubts, these woes disappeared, gone, blown out of her mind when she was on all fours beneath Alvin.

The best part was how much pleasure he got from her. Always grateful. Always passionate. Something that could not be faked.

She believed she deserved the pain she felt. The pain that gave her pleasure.

She wondered if Alvin felt the same joy with others. Who knew how many? She didn't ask. He didn't tell. Perhaps that was why she offered her taboo spot. To be different? Who knew how different she really was? Another spot would be less painful.

The thing that most drove her to tell John was that it would surely get a reaction. That was it. A reaction was uncommon. If you dress up every night, why would tonight be different? If your routine was the same every day, what was there to talk about? A special day meant going to another beach, which wasn't much different from Long Beach Bluff. Why leave the resort? It would mean something to see a different reaction from him, an *emotional* one. Wouldn't that display his love? Was she afraid he would say or do nothing? Impossible. John was a passionate man. But as each year at the resort passed, he perhaps grew less passionate, more buried, like the damn plane just down the road that he loved to talk about.

She would have to tell him eventually. This was a secret a husband and wife should not keep. Now that he was back to his running routine, she always timed her showers for when he arrived home, which was easy, because he was so anal about time, especially when he ran. Alvin always left with plenty of margin. She knew John would come straight to the master bathroom to strip and shower. The way she hugged him, the way he hugged back when she stepped out of the stall—both soaked with moisture, one clean, the other dirty, but which one?—was the most intimate thing they shared, far more intimate than their weekend lovemaking, far more intimate than what she shared with Alvin. Each time, as she turned her head, pressed the side of her face against John's chest, felt his loving embrace, listened to the rapid beat of his heart, fought back the tears, she thought now was the time.

She had always believed that open communication in marriage was the healthiest way. But she worried that non-communication, the unhealthy choice, was sometimes the right one. What if they actually confronted all of their marital demons together? What if they truly expressed all of their dissatisfactions with life, with each other? Would John ever be the same? Would she?

She always wimped out. Like her life, the outcome was not something she could predict. And that scared her. There was so much that was scary when there was so little you controlled.

Perhaps Alvin was the only thing in her life she controlled. The time. The place. The thing she allowed him to do. The things she didn't allow him to do.

But—finally—one Sunday mid-morning, after Alvin was gone, after John had returned, after she had stepped out of the shower to embrace him—as always, she hoped the hot shower and his affection would make her clean again—instead of pulling away, grabbing a towel, heading into the bedroom, she looked up at him. When he held her like this, or when he stroked her hair at breakfast, or grazed his lips along her neck when she brushed her teeth, it was more exciting than their sex. She wanted to kiss him now more than when they laid in bed. Something about their nocturnal preludes to lovemaking, the perfunctory smooching and fondling, had already become routine. But now she noticed the deep brown of his eyes. For a moment, she believed he *saw* her more clearly than he had in a very long time.

She said, "Last time I went to Puerto Rico I had a lesion removed. They did a biopsy. It's confirmed. Skin cancer. I have to go back for more treatment. If they prescribe chemo I'll lose all my hair."

KATE & ROB-O

"Are we exclusive?" Kate asked, as Rob-O washed the dishes while she dried, after he had cooked another delicious meal, this time pepper pot, a Caribbean stew of mixed meat and spicy peppers.

"Why do you ask?"

"If we weren't living together, but dating, I would understand non-exclusivity, especially on this island. But we are under the same roof."

"Kate, you have nothing to worry about."

"Okay." She put the dried dishes away in a cabinet.

"Is this because I suggested a threesome with Sherry at the front desk?" Rob-O asked.

That night, months ago, when she'd watched Alvin and Rob-O kiss, was amazing. It was as if for one evening, well one experience, she had been gifted a different body, a miraculous one.

Weeks later the three of them tried a repeat, but this time Alvin touched Rob-O and he jerked away, ended the encounter.

She had not come since.

"No," Kate answered. "Well, yes, in a way."

"I want you to orgasm."

"Still fine without them."

"But I can't with Alvin. I mean what happened that last—"

"You do have a nice ass."

"Kate, I'd be destroyed."

She laughed. "I understand."

"Do you?"

"It was your idea to begin with."

"Not my idea how it turned out," Rob-O said.

"It was fun."

"I was happy. For you. But do you know what they call gays on Antigua?"

"Kissing Alvin for my benefit doesn't make you gay."

"*Antiman.* Yep. And I know it doesn't make me gay. But he and I still made out. And if it becomes a regular thing, word will get out. I like to think of myself as modern, somewhat liberated, more renaissance, but this place is just too small."

"That's why I haven't asked for a repeat."

"But you haven't orgasmed since."

"Yet I still love you. And live with you. And have brought up exclusivity."

"And I love you, too. Really."

"Then why the threesome with Sherry?"

Dishes done, Rob-O dried his hands, retreated to the living room, which housed a white, plush sofa and a matching love seat. He sat on the seat. Kate nuzzled next to him.

"So, you're worried I'll cheat on you?" he asked.

"I understand monogamy is hard. Perhaps humans aren't suited for it. How many long-term couples still have the hots for each other?"

"I hope we find out."

She laughed, snuggled deeper.

"I guess Twiggy and Ned prove your point," Rob-O added.

"Do you think she's still banging Alvin?"

"Who knows?"

"There are rumors even Becca and Alvin are doing the nasty," Kate said.

"You see. There are no secrets on this island, especially at Long Beach Bluff."

She wondered if he knew that Alvin had come on to her privately, invited her back to the spot without him.

"You're all man, Rob-O. That's no secret."

He was the first boyfriend she really loved. Was it because he cooked so well and so often for her? Was it because he cared so much about her pleasure and made such efforts above and beyond—even risked *antiman*—that endeared him so much to her? In some ways, he was average looking, already a slight belly, small bump in the nose. On the street passing by, or on the prowl at a club, she probably wouldn't give him a second look. But seeing him here, on the island, at the resort, most significantly at the waterfront, so damn good at everything he did, added a sexiness to his already interesting personality. She watched him when he occasionally showed off his water-skiing prowess: tricks with the rope, one-skiing, barefoot skiing. And, as she did, he loved to teach, whether it was a little kid, or an old lady, whether it was scuba diving, sailing, water-skiing, or fishing, he was good at it all, and approached every lesson with the same robust joy.

And it made him handsome. In her eyes. And in the eyes of many of the women who arrived as tourists—or worked at the resort.

And he was funny. He made a promise to make her laugh at least once a day. He more than delivered: crazy dance moves, snuck into her classes, imitated Ned's puffy cheeks when he lost his temper over more trivial nonsense. Came up with pet names for his penis. Gave it opinions with the high voice of a silly cartoon character.

He made this place paradise.

"Kate, I brought up the threesome with Sherry because I'd be more comfortable making out with her while you watched and got off."

She looked carefully at him. "I don't think I'd have the same reaction. I'd be too jealous. Something about you kissing Alvin made it purely voyeuristic. There was never a belief this could get in the way of our relationship."

"And you think Sherry would?"

"She's so hot! You know she was in last year's beauty pageant at Carnival. Her boobs are huge!"

"I know."

She slapped him lightly on the arm. "You see. I'm jealous already."

"I could find out if Alvin and Twiggy are still going at it and we can make a clandestine visit to The Spot."

"Too risky."

"I agree," Rob-O said. "But you know I do have my eye on Juanita, the elderly lady who sells trinkets on the beach."

"You making out with Juanita would absolutely be no problem. Just don't expect an orgasm."

"Then I'll pass."

"Good."

They laughed, kissed deeply, held each other. He played with her nipples. She touched his penis, then whispered, "Big Pedro's arrived for a visit."

"Big Pedro may be a *slight* exaggeration."

She pulled his hand to the moistness between her legs. "Petite Paulina disagrees."

They laughed some more. Kissed again.

He said, "You've inspired me to make the concrete *decision* to be only with you."

She said, "You've helped me accept the *imperfection* of my unwarranted jealousy."

She took his hand, led him to the bedroom, added, "Maybe because monogamy's so hard it adds value to relationships that live by it."

NED & TWIGGY

ON MONDAY:

Ned had a little time because Twiggy already departed for breakfast. He lifted the phone receiver by the bed in the guest room, laid flat on his back, head propped up on two fluffy pillows. He dialed a number in town. A woman answered the phone.

"Hello, Raven," Ned said. "Hope it's not too early. Was yesterday a late night, sweetheart?"

"I always have time for you, lover," Raven replied.

"I'm wearing just underwear."

"Leave it on. I want you to reach into your shorts this time, like the dirty schoolboy you are."

"I am a dirty schoolboy, aren't I?"

"Yes. If your mother finds out, she'll give you a good spanking."

"No one can find out, right, Raven?"

"Not as long as you're a good boy."

"And what do I have to do to be a good boy?"

"Listen to Raven."

"I always do."

"And send an extra tip."

"I will."

"Close your eyes." He complied. "Imagine I'm there, undressing for you."

"Yes." His breathing was already erratic.

"I reveal my full breasts and my chocolate nipples."

"Oh, yes."

"I drop my skirt and you see my pretty sheer panties."

A moan this time.

"You want to touch me?" she asked.

"Yes, Raven, I do."

"Slide your hand under the elastic of your boxers and do everything I tell you."

"Yes, mistress."

It didn't take long. It never did with Raven. She was always good for an easy quick one. He loved her voice. She knew just what to say. She made him feel how much she wanted him.

ON TUESDAY:

It was later in the morning. He had more time these days because John did such a good job. Twiggy was on her way into St. John's to purchase a birthday present for Leona, the head laundry lady, so he could go at his own relaxed pace without worry or interruption.

Also, Full Moon Bay would have a crowd of guests.

He went to the balcony that faced the Atlantic where his telescope was situated to study stars at night, which he never did. He moved it to the other side of the house, just behind the sliding glass door that opened to the balcony that faced the bay. He closed the curtains, aligned the telescope so it pointed towards the beach, positioned the long tube part between the two curtains so only the lens was visible from the outside, not that the balcony was easy to see, only the tennis court was below it, and it was empty, and Full Moon was at least seventy yards away.

Ned crouched behind the telescope eyepiece, searched the shoreline until he found a group of thirty-something women in skimpy bikinis. He zoomed the lens in, then dropped his shorts and underwear, kept his tee shirt on. He could've set this up before he got dressed and done the deed naked. But it seemed dirtier this way, reminding him of when he was a youngster at the resort and spied through the window in his dad's bedroom that faced the Atlantic side beach. He finished into a fistful of tissues to keep the clean-up simple, then moved the telescope back to its original position.

ON WEDNESDAY:

Twiggy met with friends for lunch at another resort. He locked the front door from the inside in case the maid returned. He found Twiggy's panties in the hamper: cream-colored, skimpy, silky, his favorite. They were at the top of the hamper, so he believed she wore them yesterday. He retreated to their bed this time, laid down on his half, on the pillows, closed his eyes, pressed her panties to his nostrils, breathed deeply. It was like she was there. It was like when they were first married. Her scent was intoxicating. He tasted her. It didn't get any dirtier than this; the taboo of it all aroused him more than the real thing. It did not take him long to finish.

ON THURSDAY:

Not much time. Twiggy was about to leave for breakfast in the main dining room. He had a meeting with John and the head chef to discuss next week's menu and what purchases needed to be made. Most of the food they served, aside from local fish, mango, pineapple, bananas, some choice vegetables, came from off island. But he needed to get off. It cleared his head. Relaxed him. It was a very distinct high, one that needed variety to maintain a certain pleasure level, so the endorphins could flood his brain, give him a brief but enjoyable rush, for a moment he was not so old.

He rarely achieved full erection anymore, even at climax, but it still felt great; he still produced fluid, as he had since puberty.

"Go down without me, Twiggy. I'll be along shortly."

She obliged. She wore white pants, three-quarter length down her legs. "Pedal pushers," she called them. And a sheer white blouse over her bathing suit top. She had on an oversized straw hat and large sunglasses, always careful to wear sunblock and avoid overexposure to the brutal Antigua sun.

He gave it a few minutes, then went to his home office, unlocked a cabinet, dug deep behind folders until he came up with a magazine called *BABES IN PARADISE*. All nude, bought by Alvin, secretly transferred to Ned. He lately thought to add more variety by purchasing a VCR and TV monitor, like Rob-O had at the waterfront. Ned had heard about the video side business at the grocery in St. John's. But he wanted Long Beach Bluff to remain TV free. He wasn't good at electronic stuff. Not as easy to avoid getting caught if he watched a video. Nothing better than an old school nudie magazine.

He went to the guest bathroom, locked the door behind him, dropped his shorts, leafed through the pages, searched for his favorite photos. The pic would have to be different from last week in order to achieve his daily goal. The phone rang in the master bedroom. Too far along to talk to anyone. The ringing stopped. Ah there…Miss Jamaica, in full, smooth, ebony glory. He glossed over the multiple shots of her front and back, studied her, re-memorized her curves, imprinted her in his psyche as if he prepared for an important exam, the strength in his hand an empowerment he wanted to make last.

KNOCK! KNOCK! KNOCK!

"Ned, why are you in the guest bathroom?" Twiggy asked. "And why's the door locked? John wants you to bring down the invoices from last month's food purchases."

This was the worst scenario for being caught. He only called Raven when Twiggy was gone. Plus he left the bedroom door open so he could hear her come in downstairs. All he would have to do is pull up his shorts and hang up. With the telescope, he could always say he was setting up for an eastern view of the sky for later tonight.

But now he was in a panic. Nowhere to run or hide.

"I'm on the can!" he barked.

He pulled up his shorts—his erection already shrunk to normal size—discreetly opened the cabinet under the sink and hid *BABES IN PARADISE* behind spare towels. He took one more deep breath, put on his best business face.

Maybe he was extra red; his cheeks too often gave away his emotions. Maybe she heard the opening of the cabinet door. Maybe she was naturally suspicious because he was in the guest bathroom and had locked the door. Maybe it was because he couldn't make eye contact as he opened the door and nervously tried to shuffle past her. Maybe it was because he never flushed the toilet! Or maybe it was simply because he opened his mouth and said, "The master... toilet...was clogged."

"You were jerking off, weren't you?" He was about to defend when she added, after a quick sniff, "When you're on the can, half the resort takes off towards the bay."

"I..."

Her hand flew up to cover her face as she said, "No, I don't want to know. I'm out of here." She turned to exit.

He should've let her go. It would be less embarrassing, and he would have time to move the magazine back to its hiding place.

But the thing he hated most was when someone dismissed him *and* walked away, just like his mother had done, leaving him behind on this island as a fourteen-year-old with a father who had only one other focus aside from Long Beach Bluff: drinking.

He listened to the click of her heeled sandals on the tiled floor that led up to the front door then yelled downstairs, "I need some way to get off while living with a frigid bitch!"

He hoped to hear the door slam behind her. He was not in the mood for a major argument. He had made his point.

But the click came back towards him. He went downstairs to meet it and they ended up circling each other in the living room, around the three-piece sofa unit, like two rams about to butt horns.

"You stopped touching me a long time ago," she said, as she tried to keep her voice under control, but her anxiety slipped through anyway.

He collapsed on the sofa. Already exhausted. Too old for this battle.

"All right," he said. "We're going to do this. Now. I know it's been building in both of us. Maybe we're still together because we avoided it. But nothing's stopping us now."

She sat opposite him, arms crisscrossed against her chest, each on a short couch that was part of the three-sided square arrangement, the long couch marking the ample distance between them.

He said, "I need more from you than beautiful."

"What do you mean?"

"The legs, the body, the pretty face just doesn't inspire the same reaction."

"Can you imagine my reaction to your beer belly and hair loss?"

"You never want to do anything kinky. You never touch my butt. I'm not allowed to touch yours. You're way too vanilla."

"Remember the time I wore the cheerleader outfit you asked for?"

"That was fun."

"It was like I wasn't even there. As if you bought only one ticket to some teenage fantasy."

"There's different pressure on guys. Women can appear to be the same whether aroused or not."

"Can't fake a lack of lubrication."

"You wrote it off to aging."

"How many handjobs and blowjobs have I given you in the last fifteen years?"

"Sometimes that's just easier."

"But what about me? What about touching me, or going down on me?"

"Not easy when you're not that turned on."

"And it is for women?"

"Twiggy, one thing you have to understand. A guy feels a lot of pressure to perform. You can't hide the failure of a limp penis."

"Agreed."

"What do you mean by that?"

"Just agreeing."

"You see that's it right there. I can stand most anything: name calling, selfishness, lack of kindness, even meanness. But I can't stand denunciation."

"Neither can I."

A silence. Both regrouped for Round Two.

Finally, Ned said, "Aging is fucked up in so many ways. Sexually, I still have the same urges in my mind. A nice ass. Pretty tits. I never stop looking. I can still imagine seducing that person, somehow getting her in bed, giving her the night of her life. But the reality is, I don't believe I could even if I had the opportunity. It became difficult even when you stimulated me. All I have left is the daily wank."

"Daily?" Her voice rose with surprise.

"Yeah. Hard to imagine, huh? But I still like to get off. It feels great. For a brief moment, I'm knocking on being single again instead of pushing sixty."

"You are pushing sixty."

"I'm well aware."

"And you're not single."

"I can promise that I've never slept with another woman since we've been married."

"Truthfully, I'm surprised," Twiggy said. "You've been absent for so many unsensual years."

"Truthfully," Ned said. "I'm not even sure I could with you, or with anyone if the chance arose. It's easier for me to stay away than fail. I can orgasm, but it's never fully erect anymore and only stays mildly hard with the constant stimulation of a rapid hand."

"More information than I need."

"Erectile malfunction."

"Dysfunction."

"Malfunction."

Twiggy uncrossed her arms.

Ned took a deep breath, took her in completely, something he rarely did anymore. He muttered, "Don't I get points for being monogamous? You could've married a Lothario or someone like Alvin who can't keep his dick in his pants."

She took her own deep breath, turned, looked through the back glass doors, out to sea.

"You get points for sitting down and talking to me like a person," Twiggy said. "Especially when you live such an unexamined life."

"What's that supposed to mean?"

"I believe it's the only way you could be so brusque with people who piss you off, so tough on the staff, so into what your needs are, what you want, never asking about mine. I wonder if you ever look at anything from any other point of view aside from your own. I doubt you ever take stock of your actions. Evaluate what you do. Ponder changes. I assume that's the only way someone could be you. And it's probably the same reason why Alvin can't keep his dick in his pants."

"Are you speaking from experience?"

She turned to meet his stare, said, "I can promise you I've never slept with Alvin."

"If he wasn't so good at managing local politics and staff issues while helping to meet the local quota, I probably would've fired his ass a long time ago."

She stood up, said, "From now on I'll make a lot of noise if I come back to the house unexpectedly."

He countered with, "I won't say anything more about your sleeping habits."

Then he got up, left the room. His voice trailed back to her. "I wish we could've had that kid."

SEPTEMBER 25, 1989

One week after Hugo swept through Antigua, Detective Reggie sat at his desk and read Alvin's autopsy report. Antigua's lone medical examiner, Dr. Richardson, a greying, older man, sat patiently in front of the desk in a white medical jacket and black slacks, on a plain metal chair. When Reggie finished reading, he slid his glasses to the top of his forehead and asked, "Murda or accident?"

"As the report reads," Dr. Richardson said, "I can't be sure. The throat wound seems to be more of a puncture than a slash."

"You give a broad time of death."

"It's difficult to pinpoint. The storm conditions could've reduced the body temperature at a faster rate. I'm estimating some time when the storm hit full force and twelve hours before."

Reggie studied the document again.

"Do you have any theories?" Dr. Richardson asked.

"The body coulda floated up from the bay, or dumped at the spot by the gate, or even blown there by the storm. Or it all coulda gone down right at the spot. There seemed to be several footprints around the body, but because of the storm and those who found him, I can't identify whose footprints they are and when they made. After recheckin the photos, I see a pair of prints right by the gate—big foot, like Alvin—facin the resort, that look deeper in the ground."

"Deeper?"

"Like maybe someone climb over the gate and that's where he jump down."

"Did Alvin have a key to the lock?"

"Yankee say only him have the key."

"Any suspects?"

"The whole group look suspicious to me," Reggie said with a laugh. "Them women look brokenhearted. I also found a note on Long Beach Bluff stationery warnin Alvin to stay away from some gyal. I'm going there today for handwritin samples."

"Not easy investigating the White Man."

"If he guilty, I find him."

The resort looked better. Electricity was back in some areas on the island. Limited phone service. The airport was open, but not yet fully functional, and accepted only a few official flights. Ned faxed in a claim and his insurance would cover the bulk of repairs. Truckloads of sand began arriving, and workers carted it from the trucks to the Atlantic side beach—the aftermath waves still high and rough—raked it smooth, melded it with the muddy sand left from the storm. Much of the debris, both natural and manmade, had been removed. The new roof on Building One showed progress, some rooms ready for occupancy in the other buildings. Ned considered taking reservations for early November. Other resorts would probably not be open by Christmas. The waiters were kept on salary, as they helped with the cleaning and reconstruction. The next major order of business was the roof at the beach bar and then repairs to the boat dock.

Each day, John circulated around the resort, made sure the resurrection went smoothly.

Twiggy spent a lot of her time in Old Hill Village. More got done if she made calls and handled business personally, especially with the government. She sent out a mailing to the resort list, asking for hurricane disaster donations to her fund. The holes in the street had widened considerably from the heavy rain and the main road was barely passable. Houses needed repair. The school needed to replace wet books and warped desks. But the electricity was back, and she had food and water essentials trucked in two days after Hugo hit. Road repair would begin later in the week, thanks to her persistence and personal relationship with the minister in charge. The fund would be depleted soon, unless someone rich stepped up, but she was determined that Old Hill would look better than ever.

Rob-O and Kate spent their time at the waterfront, raked the sand, disposed of the wet wood from the roof, repaired the bar with the waterfront staff, got the boats ready. When more wood arrived, they'd begin work on the bar roof and the dock. Rob-O had already done a thorough snorkel to assess the dock damage. It had collapsed in certain areas, but was fixable.

Ned mostly stayed in the main office, surrounded by multiple phones, giant copy and fax machines, and a large, wood mailbox unit, with numerous cubbies, for sorting employee and guest mail. On the opposite wall hung the resort's first dry erase board, one that replaced the old chalkboard which charted month-to-month reservations and room assignments. Ned took pride in assuming he was the first person on the island with a dry erase board, discovered at last year's hotel convention in Miami, and shipped in specially this past summer. There was a separate office for the accountant, who lived off site and had skedaddled to New York once he got word that Hugo might hit the leeward islands. But he was back at work, a small man with tiny round glasses, who dealt with invoice after invoice, as he sorted things out for insurance claims. Broken glass from the many windows around the property was perhaps the biggest obstacle to reopening. The staff had completely scraped away and cleaned up the smashed boutique window, but they still could not get the glazier to come in, as he was busy all over the island and ran low on inventory.

The office was where Reggie found Ned, who sat behind his desk, busy with papers, after the secretary had pointed the detective in.

"Afternoon, sir," Reggie said. He carried a worn, black leather briefcase. "Makin splendid progress around the property."

"And thus quite busy," Ned answered without standing or looking up.

Reggie studied the resort owner, waited patiently for him to make eye contact.

Finally, while still glancing down at the papers he held in his hand, Ned said, "How can I help you?"

"I need a handwritin sample."

"Whose?"

"Yours."

"What the fuck for?"

"Part of the Alvin investigation."

Ned put the papers down. Now Reggie had his full attention.

"Are you fucking kidding me?"

"Just a formality."

"So you want a sample from everyone on the property?"

"Just the ones around when the terrible thing happened."

"Are you saying I'm a suspect?"

"Doin my due diligence."

"Well, you can take your due diligence out of my office and off the property. Now. Come back with a subpoena or warrant or whatever you'll need. Because I'm certainly not obliging." He picked the papers back up. "And don't forget I'm in tight with the PM."

"The Prime Minister a good man, Mr. Ned."

"You know I'm paying for Alvin's funeral."

"You or Miss Twiggy?"

"What's that supposed to mean?"

"I hear she's a generous soul."

Ned's face darkened. He said, "Just let me know when you're releasing the body."

"Should be soon."

Ned seemed to think they were done, but Reggie persisted with, "Will you be attendin the funeral, sir?"

"Unlikely. Half the women on Antigua will probably be there."

"Who you think go from Long Beach Bluff?"

"Is that another question like the one asking for a handwriting sample?"

"Important to know who'll miss him the most."

"Time for you to go, Reggie."

Reggie pulled out his business card from an inside jacket pocket, stood in his spot, held it towards Ned with an extended arm, said, "In case you change your mind."

Ned had no choice but to get up and sidestep to the front of his desk to accept the card. Just as Ned reached for the card it slipped from Reggie's hand. The two men stared at each other, head-on, the business card between them. Neither made a move.

Finally, Ned bent down and Reggie watched him pick up the card with his left hand. Reggie turned to leave, but not before he added, "I'll be back if I don't have luck elsewhere."

He closed the door behind him before Ned could respond.

At the waterfront, Rob-O, hammer in hand, repaired wood picnic benches that were too heavy to be warehoused during the storm. As weighty as they were, Hugo had tossed them around like tree branches, some all the way to the patio. Kate hammered in new nails as well, on a nearby bench.

"How are you today, Mr. Rob-O?" Reggie asked as he approached from the exit road.

"Me yah," Rob-O answered as he looked up from his work.

Reggie smiled. "So you up on the local patois I see."

"Antigua's home for me."

Reggie looked over at Kate as she hammered. He asked Rob-O, "Mind takin a walk with me?"

Kate smiled politely.

"Am I under arrest?" Rob-O asked.

"Not yet."

They both laughed.

Rob-O put the hammer down, wiped the sweat from his palms on his cargo shorts. The pair headed towards the beach, made a right at the dock, walked along the bay away from the resort buildings. At an isolated table with a broken beach umbrella, Reggie sat first, followed by Rob-O. Reggie dug into his briefcase, produced plain white paper and a pen.

"I need a writin sample, Mr. Rob-O."

Surprised, Rob-O said with a nervous smile, "I really am a suspect?"

"Just a formality."

"Something you want me to write?"

"*Stay away from her. Or there will be consequences.*"

"That's very specific."

"You asked."

Rob-O took the pen, scribbled on the paper with his right hand. He didn't get all the words correctly, but it was close enough. Reggie studied the handwriting, then took out the Long Beach Bluff stationery note found in Alvin's house, compared the two.

Rob-O's childlike scrawl wasn't even close.

"So I'm in the clear?" Rob-O asked with a wide grin.

"How well did you know Alvin?"

"We shared beers from time to time."

"Anything else?"

Rob-O shifted nervously in his chair. "Are you asking if we shared anything else?"

"I mean did you keep company off the property?"

"No."

"Was Alvin friendly with Kate?"

"What do you mean?

"Friends with her. Like with you. Maybe sharin a few beers."

"No."

Reggie couldn't help but notice Rob-O squirm. He reached back into the briefcase, pulled out the broken liquor bottle half-wrapped in a thick towel, whisked the towel off, showed it to Rob-O, asked, "What can you tell me bout this?"

"Judging from what's left of the label, it's a broken rum bottle."

"The one I found near Alvin's body."

Rob-O looked back towards Kate, who stopped working and stared down the beach at both of them. "I really should get back to work."

"Did you lock up all the liquor bottles before the storm?"

"Yes."

"Do you think maybe Alvin was drinkin from it?"

"How would I know?"

"Toxicology report shows no alcohol in the system."

"The bottle could've floated on shore from the bay, batted around by the storm."

"Distinct possibility, except when a bottle is batted around it usually shatters. This one broken, like someone had hold of the neck and smashed the bottom against a rock." Brief pause. "Or the side of a bar, maybe."

"Do I need a lawyer?"

"Do you?"

"No," Rob-O said, as he stared out to sea.

There was a longer pause.

"Did you find any blood on the bottle?" Rob-O asked.

"If there was," Reggie answered, "it got well-washed by the storm."

"Does the pointy end match the wound on Alvin's neck?"

"Hard to tell."

Another silence.

"Mr. Rob-O, is there somethin you want to tell me?"

"Is there something you know about me and Alvin and that's why you're here, asking for some bogus writing sample?"

"I really did find a threatenin letter at Alvin's house."

"But you know I didn't write it?"

"I'm sure you didn't write it. The handwritin not even close, plus the person who wrote this is left-handed."

"How do you know?"

"The way the words slant to the right."

"So why are you still questioning me?"

"I'm not singling you out, sir," said Reggie, in a more formal tone. "Just following up with the people closest to the situation."

"You getting writing samples from the women, too?"

Reggie smiled. "Don't think the women up for it, but you never know. They may have good reason too. But the note reference stayin away from a woman."

"Maybe Alvin was involved with someone's lesbian lover."

"Could be." Reggie chuckled. "That stuff more in the open now then back in my day." He searched the deep blue of Rob-O's eyes. Rob-O wiped beads of sweat from his brow with his right wrist. "But hard to keep that kind a secret on this island."

Rob-O jerked away from the detective's gaze.

Reggie re-wrapped the bottle in the towel, asked, "Things good with you and Miss Kate?"

"Things are great."

"You two live together, right?"

"I didn't kill Alvin."

"So you know nuthin about the bottle?"

"Any fingerprints on it?"

"Hardly."

"Know nothing about it."

Reggie was too old or the day was too hot for all the walking around the property he did to find John. Sweat poured down the sides of his face, dripped off his chin. He wished he had brought his hat. Finally, he asked Sherry at the front desk to page John on the walkie-talkie. Reggie waited in the shade of the open, covered lobby. Ned exited his office, gave Reggie a *you still here?* look, but remained silent.

"Hello, Detective Reggie," John said as he bounded up the steps into the lobby.

"Where you get your energy, Youngblood?"

"Still training for the race at Carnival."

"Do you have an office, someplace private?"

John could not hide his curious reaction. "Let's sit under the flamboyant tree by the patio."

They each sat in a chair, a small round table between them. The flamboyant was still shy of leaves because of the storm, but had enough branches to provide some shade.

"How's the investigation going?" John asked. "We have a special memorial planned."

"That's nice of you. The body will be released soon."

"Alvin was a fixture at Long Beach Bluff. Worked here since he was a teen."

"I remember." From his briefcase, Reggie pulled out the pen and plain white paper. "I need a handwritin sample."

Without hesitation, John said, "Of course," and reached for the pen with his left hand.

"Anything special you want me to write?"

"*Stay away from her. Or there will be consequences.*"

John paused, then shifted the pen to his right hand, was about to form the first letters, awkwardly, when he put the pen down and said, "I wrote it."

"Wrote what?"

"The note to Alvin. You must have found it at his house."

"Why did you write it?"

John took a deep breath, looked around the patio area, glad they were alone.

"We're keeping a low profile about this, as per Becca's wishes." He focused back on Reggie. "Not too long ago she had a lesion removed from the back of her neck, which turned out to be cancerous."

"Sorry to hear that, Mr. John."

"You can call me John." He lowered his voice even more when he added, "We were back and forth to Puerto Rico. Fortunately, she didn't need chemo, but the oncologist prescribed several radiation treatments and another round of scraping. Twiggy's the only one I talked to about it. I don't think anyone else knows. Unless she told Ned."

"Why wouldn't she?"

"They don't converse much. Friendly around the property, but the wind often carries their…*discussions* down the bluff to our open windows."

"Not surprisin. But wouldn't Ned wonder why you and your wife goin to Puerto Rico?"

"I told him Becca had a sick relative."

"He bought it?"

John nodded.

Reggie added, "Ned must be gullible or you're a good fibbah."

"He doesn't really care. As long as I get the job done. Which I do."

"So back to your wife and the note."

"This is just between me and you, right? Becca's a bit freaked out about the whole thing. Feeling very vulnerable. Took some time before she even told me about the diagnosis."

"She okay now?"

"In remission. Thank God. It doesn't seem to have spread anywhere else. She'll follow up every six months for at least two years."

John drummed his fingers, a signal he hoped ended the conversation. But Detective Reggie asked, "Why you going to write the sample right-handed?"

"What do you mean?"

"The note written left-handed."

"I panicked."

"So why don't you tell me why you wrote this particular note, one with a warnin."

John took his deepest breath yet. He hunched closer to Reggie, his voice now a whisper.

"You absolutely cannot breathe a word of this to a soul. Unless of course you're using it for evidence for something. I understand. But it's not evidence. Just a plea." John slowed down his breathing.

Reggie waited for John to continue.

"About a year ago I came back early from a training run and caught Alvin and my wife in bed together. They didn't see me. I was too shocked to say anything and left the house, finished the run. I wanted to say something when I returned, but she seemed very upset, scared, I think crying. I kept tabs on them both, close enough so I'm sure at least Alvin, and maybe Becca were suspicious, so I became pretty confident they stopped. It's not like Alvin can't find someone else, or multiple elses."

"So you thought it best not to say somethin?"

"I'm ashamed to say, *yes*," his voice cracked. "I was afraid it would ruin our marriage. I mean how do you come back from something like that? Do you want something to drink? My throat's parched."

"Water please. Much appreciated."

John went into the main kitchen, returned with two blue plastic tumblers of cold water. He sat. They sipped. Reggie waited patiently.

"I believed that if I confronted her," John continued, "she would be in a completely defensive position. And from that position, I didn't know what she would say....Do you understand?"

"Yessir."

"I love her. I want to stay married to her. I guess, well, I probably didn't want to hear what she had to say. If she said she didn't love me then there's no way I could go on."

"Do you think she doesn't?"

"I think she does. We've grown closer since her diagnosis. I accompanied her on every trip to Puerto Rico."

"Each marriage has its own thing that work. I'm married thirty years to my missus. We can go days without more than a *thank you, I tired, how the children?*"

"Don't get me wrong," John said. "I think husbands and wives should be honest. But sometimes you can't risk it. Saying the thing that must be said. But without knowing where it will lead. The whole thing might blow up. Maybe sometimes marriages work because of what's *not* said."

"More than you think," Reggie offered with a smile.

They sipped their water. John hoped they were done. But Reggie was here for a reason.

"So if you believe they stop, why the note?"

"Becca doesn't know that I know. Once she got the diagnosis, she got very depressed. I couldn't bear to think that Alvin could complicate her life anymore."

"That's it?"

John bit his lip, as if he made one last attempt to keep words from spilling out.

"I went back to training again. I shouldn't have. But I wanted our lives to be normal. This is the only time I think they could get away with it. For sure nothing went on during her treatment, but sometimes before she told me about the diagnosis—and maybe even sometimes now that she's doing better—she's so tender when I return from a run, maybe a little upset, but seemingly so grateful I came back, but very fragile. It dawned on me that maybe it wasn't over. I had to let Alvin know he needed to stay away."

"You think the note worked?"

"No idea."

"Well it's definitely over now."

"I'd rather it not be this way."

The two men glanced up at a bird who watched from the tree.

"Glad the flamboyant survived," Reggie said. "The leaves will come back."

"I should've gotten Alvin fired," John admitted. "But he's such a big part of the resort. Also, I felt responsible if it was continuing because I never stopped it in the first place."

Reggie nodded.

"So do you think it was me?" John asked.

"Don't know if I'll ever find out unless I get some physical evidence or someone confesses." John didn't meet Reggie's stare. "But several men seem to have an axe to grind."

"It could just be an accident."

"That possibility certainly there. One theory I floatin is that maybe Alvin was tryin to get to the wine cellar for shelter, climbed over the gate, slipped or got blown, came down hard and one of the gate spikes caught him in the throat. There's a set of deep footprints right on the inside of the gate. Unfortunately, any blood would be washed away on the spikes."

"That seems like a legitimate theory."

"Cept I don't understand why the head of the body facin the gate. The entrance road on a sharp incline down when you first enter the property. He would have to jump backwards to catch a spike in the throat. He woulda fallen on his back, with the head facing the rooms. But he in the direction towards the gate, as if he runnin away."

"If murders your first choice, I'll admit it's something I thought about in the heat of running, or during some obscure revenge fantasy, but would never do."

"Don't know what the first choice is. But I do know that sometimes these things are done by the ones who never thought about it."

SIX MONTHS BEFORE
THE STORM

JOHN & BECCA

John wanted tonight to be special. It had been three months since Becca shared with him her cancer diagnosis. The shock had turned the painful emotional separation inspired by her dalliance into the bitter possibility of permanent loss. He did not want to lose her to Alvin or the disease.

They dressed in their bedroom for the weekly Saturday night dance at the open patio off the main dining room. He had on his blue suit, white shirt, red tie. Becca wore a beautiful, tight fitting black dress, shoulders bare, a thin silk scarf around her neck to hide the scar just below the hairline. John's gaze lingered on the hip and buttock areas. The dress hugged the slender curves of her body, the hem short, not too short, but it still exposed her thin, graceful legs. This was the first dance she would attend since she had told him that the removed lesion was cancerous.

On their first trip to Puerto Rico for her initial radiation treatment, he took her hand in his and held it on his lap for the entire trip. The flight, on a small puddle-jumper, probably scared her as much as the treatment. He'd stopped training for the half-marathon completely, devoted every spare moment to her, down at the resort, up the bluff at their house, especially Sunday mornings when they enjoyed breakfast together on the balcony and admired the ocean view.

"We can move back to the States," he offered during their first flight. "Easier to get treatments. We can be near the best hospitals."

"I'm optimistic," she replied. "I don't want you to give up your dream job. The lymph nodes are clear. No further surgeries required."

"I really would if you wanted."

"And I love you for that."

She rested her head against his shoulder and blissfully nodded out. He liked the weight of her against his body, the warmth of her hand in his. As they made the bi-monthly flights together for treatment, he never felt so close. After each return, she was fatigued from the radiation and he bought her extra time in bed by bringing her meals from the dining hall, personally, when he easily could've sent up a waiter. With such care, he sensed a new security in her. She offered to go to Puerto Rico by herself when things got busy at Long Beach Bluff. She showed special guests around the property—travel agents, high profile tourists, government officials—when he had other pressing business to take care of, her mood lighter, her smile as pretty as it had ever been.

But he never missed a trip, and they repeated the hand holding, the head resting, each time they flew, followed by breakfast on the balcony.

She had diligently followed her oncologist's advice: stayed out of the sun, wore long pants and sleeves, her neck covered with a scarf, floppy hat on her head, sunblock on every exposed area. Because she spent so much time either in her room, or covered up outside, her skin turned sallow, and she lamented the lost Caribbean bronze of her complexion. He kissed her on the mouth one night and whispered, "Your lips are still as sweet."

And tonight was their personal celebration. She got the phone call from her doctor yesterday morning: cancer free. She didn't need to go back for another six months, and that was simply for a check-up. Two years of remission meant the cancer would probably never return.

And tonight, she displayed a renewed boldness with her bare shoulders and legs, her white skin more noticeable in the dark of night, against the black of her dress.

At the patio, when the four-piece band played the first slow dance, John reached out his hand towards his wife. She clasped her palm in his, the sensation more familiar than it had ever been. They strolled to the dance floor, still hand in hand, where over a dozen couples danced to Frank Sinatra's *Strangers in the Night*.

"You look beautiful," John said as they gracefully swayed under the flamboyant tree, the canopy of thick orange leaves above them.

They were indeed a handsome couple. John so tall and lean, Becca's lithe figure fitting snugly against the blueness of his suit.

He watched Twiggy and Ned dance not too far away. She had on heels, which made her that much taller than her husband. Both wore wispy smiles. John knew their dancing together was for show, even the smiles.

Over by the corner, near the steps going up to the main dining room, John saw Rob-O dance cheek to cheek with Kate as their bodies moved in perfect unison. John smirked at Rob-O's feeble attempt to meet the resort's dress code, as he had exchanged his cargo shorts for long khakis, the usual Hawaiian shirt accompanied by a blue tie dotted with small yellow pineapples. The couple seemed perfectly in love. Always kind to each other. They had difficulty arguing because sooner or later it ended up in giggles. Rob-O's goofy humor was a sharp contrast to Kate's deadpan but saucy delivery. They seemed like the way John had imagined things were the first year of his marriage to Becca, or maybe like how he always imagined he and his wife should be.

To lose her to another man would be a blow to his heart. To lose her to disease would be a scarring of his soul. He pulled her closer.

"I think the ladies are checking you out," Becca said.

He looked over at a group of white-haired women in floral dresses, their hair done up and set with spray this afternoon at the resort's beauty parlor. They waved. He nodded back. They returned to their chat.

"It's clear I only have eyes for you, Becca."

"You haven't lost your corniness." She kissed him on the cheek.

He spun her around twice, held her lower back as he dipped her. "You think so?" He pressed his lips to her mouth. "After three months of worry, it's time to cut loose." One more twirl, then he pulled her to him tight. "But I won't let go."

She pressed herself closer, turned her head to the side, rested against his chest, like she did when she stepped out of the shower after he returned from his runs, something she had not had to do these past three months.

"I really do love you," Becca intoned.

"And I love you."

"But I don't deserve you."

"You're the one who gave up your dreams to support my career," John said.

"Not sure I had any dreams."

"Do you now?"

"Yes." She looked up at him. "To stay healthy and safe. In your arms."

They left the dance early. The closeness of her body, the texture of her skin as it touched his, her heat against him, had released the intense desire that he buried these months during her quest to get healthy again. No sex, no running, no outlets. He maintained discipline—another reason he was good at his job—focused on his wife and her health. He even passed on opportunities for self-pleasure, though the release would've been welcomed, but he wanted to display his deepest loyalties during this time, though she would have had no clue either way. Any personal indulgence would've felt like a guilty betrayal during a time when someone so young was coming face to face with thoughts of mortality.

Back at their bedroom they scrambled to remove their clothes. But before they got into bed, Becca made a move towards the bathroom to brush her teeth. John grabbed her gently by the wrist, said, "No. You don't have to. I don't care. I just want to be in bed with you."

There was a slight hesitation. He knew her preference. But she kissed him deeply while they slipped under the sheets. Kissing that did not stop! Her hands ran the length of his body, touched him, delicately, at his nipples, along the inside of his thighs. It felt like the night of their honeymoon. At this same resort. Before employment.

Everything about being with her in bed made him happy. Her desire for him, the physicality of their touches, their licks, their sucking, their kisses brought a welcome relief after three sedentary months. She lay on her back in the missionary position, his favorite, waited, and he wanted to enter her more than anything in the world. But he gently turned Becca onto her stomach, grasped a hip in each hand, and lifted her onto all fours. He so wanted to please her. He wanted her to feel him deeply, his desire for her.

From behind, as he touched her vaginal opening, he asked, "Is it okay if I do it this way?"

"If you want to," she whispered, head straight, as she spoke towards the headboard.

He looked at the surgical scar that dotted the back of her neck. "I want to make you happy. Any way you want. With me."

"I am happy."

"I want you to want me."

"I do want you."

Her tone did not match the luster of the evening. He raised his penis higher, touched her other opening. "Do you want it here?"

She quickly squirmed out from under him, onto her back, looked up into his eyes, reached for his shoulders, pulled him to her, said, "Make love to me the way you always do. I miss it so much."

And he did. They thrashed and moaned, face to face, barriers unlocked, desire escaped, as they matched each other's warmth and came together.

He collapsed onto his back, breathed heavier than usual since it had been so long without exercise. She rolled into him, onto her side, head at his shoulder, as her lungs expanded and receded with her recovery.

"Lovely," she gasped.

"Pleasing you means more than anything."

"Oh, John, I don't think there's a woman alive who wouldn't want to be with you, especially our guests, especially if they could see your kind heart."

He laughed it off, then said, "You wanting me is enough."

"I do. I really do. I've been so selfish, these last few months especially. No one could be more caring and tender than you've been."

He did not respond. The silence allowed him to enjoy her words.

"I need you to be happy, too," she added. "It can't all be about me. You need to follow your passions. Please, it's not really a problem. Especially now that I'm so much better." She picked her head up, kissed him on the cheek, and whispered,

"I want you to start running again."

ROB-O & KATE

It had been almost six months since Kate had the one and only orgasm of her life, out on the beach, under the bluff, as she watched Alvin and him make out. Rob-O was disappointed they did not have another breakthrough. He ran out of special things to do on Wednesdays, especially after Kate had axed the threesome with Sherry. Sometimes Kate sensed his frustration and asked him to please forget about it, that it had nothing to do with him, or the size of his penis, it was just how she was built, and she enjoyed everything they did.

Their relationship was mostly good. It was mostly great. It was good even when he had thoughts in the back of his mind about something lacking in him, her, both. It was great when he could forget completely about her inability to orgasm.

He remembered those months after college, some fifteen years ago, when he was the first mate on his buddy's sailboat, the pair of them island hopping, docking in some bay, taking the motorized dinghy to shore, finding a night spot, having yet another practically anonymous encounter with a local or visiting hottie. Practically anonymous because he always shared his real first name. Practically anonymous because he shared little else aside from his body. There were no conversations about what he planned to do with his life, what he studied, what his ambitions were. Sailing the Caribbean on a boat with your best bud was the easiest place, the simplest way to be completely without ambition.

But then on yet another deep blue, Caribbean sunny day—he and his pal spread out on their backs atop lounge cushions splayed along the deck, without clothes, the wind in the sails and his shaggy blond hair, while they nursed one beer after another—Rob-O's friend asked, "What makes the perfect relationship for you?"

Rob-O thought seriously for a moment. If it was back in the haze of college, he would probably answer *having great sex with a babe and then afterwards she turned into a pizza.* It would be a stupid thing to say now. It was a stupid thing to think back then. He had been stupid. He was still stupid. Because all he could answer was, "I never really thought about it, bro'."

"I have," his friend said, his entire body tanned without lines, black hair also long and shaggy, heavy black beard thick and scruffy.

They took extra long sips of their beers. More silence. Rob-O closed his eyes. It was as if the question had never been asked.

But then his buddy spoke up again, confidently, prepared to maximize the execution of his words.

"The perfect relationship is one you can't find until you're older, because even in college, even after college, we're all dumb shits who think with our dicks."

Rob-O grunted agreement. That was probably why he had such small thoughts.

"So there has to be a point," the captain of the ship continued, "when you grow old enough, or become smart enough to understand that getting drunk, getting high, having great sex, rotating partners, partying all night to just the right music is not enough."

"Sounds good to me," Rob-O mumbled, already drunk in the midday heat. Both of them already drunk.

"That's because you're not there yet. Neither am I. But I'm getting closer. I needed this trip for perspective, to indulge in my hardiest appetites before settling down to a real job and embarking upon the sincere search for someone to share my life with, someone who has the potential to be a primo wife and mother."

"So, you formulated this theory of the perfect relationship while on this jaunt?"

"*Jaunt*. Excellent choice of words," slurred his buddy. "Yes. I'm having a fantastic time. I wouldn't want to be anywhere else. I wouldn't want to be with anyone else. But I also have time and space to think about the future."

"You mean like tomorrow?"

"I mean like what happens when this trip is done, and I have to return the boat to my dad."

"Wow. I wasn't sure there was going to be an end to this trip."

"You actually inspired my hypothesis."

"That's a word I haven't heard since tenth grade geometry."

"You may be thinking *hypotenuse*."

"Maybe."

"Anyway, of course one's significant other should have the looks, the smarts, and the sense of humor, but what I think we all really need to make it last in the long term, is to find someone who isn't just one more person to *deal* with when you get home from work."

"Work?"

"Whatever job we do...*or whatever time we waste*—"

"That sounds more like me," Rob-O said.

"We'll get to you in a minute. Just let me get this theory out. Ah, another geometry word."

"Go for it."

"Think about it. We're all doomed on some level, some more, some less, to dealing with shit at our jobs. Lousy boss, moody co-workers, hectic commute, fucked up clients."

"I'm fucked up right now."

"Me too. But I'm going to see this through." He took a long swig of beer, finished the bottle, tossed it into a pile below their feet, and reached for another in an ice-filled cooler of Budweisers. "There's no escaping the bullshit of the world."

"Unless you're on a sailboat somewhere in the Caribbean without a fucking care."

"Exactly. The person you settle down with. Your significant other. Has to be like this trip. This person can't be another anchor in the daily doldrums of life. This person must be so cool she untethers you and allows you to sail free."

Rob-O propped up, leaned on his elbows behind him, feet straight out in front. "And I somehow inspired this theory or hypothesis?"

"Yes. Because having you here makes this trip perfect. You're never moody."

"At least out at sea."

"We only have fun. You don't say stupid shit. Or if you do, it's funny. You don't hassle me about anything, like why don't I trim my beard, comb my hair, cut my nails, stop drinking so much, do more of the work when we come about in the heavy winds."

"You could actually do more work."

"See, you never complained. You're hassle free. You're making this post-college time an awesome experience. The perfect relationship is all of this with the right honey."

They thought for a while, quiet, as each pondered the essence of this equation, until Rob-O piped in with, "I think you're absolutely 100 percent correct. Having a significant other who makes a trip like this even better and is not just one more narrow-minded, narcissistic bimbo is absolute perfection. You're a mathematical genius."

"Thank you. Compliments at just the right time makes it that much better."

And now, all this time later in Antigua, behind the wheel of his beat-up Datsun, as he drove on the wrong side of the road—

if he were back in the States—Rob-O realized that, according to the hypothesis formulated and perfected that day on the boat, Kate was absolutely *not* someone else he had to deal with. Not like John when he was in a hurry. Not like Ned every minute of the day. Not like Yankee when you disturbed his nap. Not like Alvin who only thought of himself. Not like Becca who sometimes walked by without saying hello (was it him or was it her?). And not like Twiggy who was super sweet, but too often sad. Kate was almost always in a good mood. If she wasn't, he couldn't tell. She didn't put up with his shit, but approached any criticism of him without a trace of vindictiveness. He must get on her nerves sometimes. But he couldn't tell. The worst was probably her teasing humor. And that always made him laugh. Her worst thing made him laugh! He truly believed she loved him. He knew he loved her. He was thrilled to work so closely with her every day. He was ecstatic to share a bed with her at night. They both loved kids. Kate, very simply, was the ideal woman for the perfect relationship, his free-flowing, sun on his face, wind in his hair, sail.

With just one, no he couldn't call it an imperfection, just one slight bump in the road.

Which was why he used his spare time—on this Wednesday afternoon lunch break—to drive into St. John's to the video store.

He parked around the corner from Moody's Grocery Store. No sense raising anyone's suspicions by taking a spot on the same street. The store had a big front window full of home products like dishes, pots, pans, detergent. He entered, silently cursing the jingle of the bells above the door that caused the few local shoppers, who strolled the vegetable and cereal aisles, to glance his way. He told himself not to be nervous. No one could possibly know why he was here, except Moody, but he wouldn't know exactly why this time was different. Nevertheless, when he eased past Moody—who was at the register—a short, dark-skinned Indian man with a pencil thin moustache—and slipped through the curtain next to the banana bin that led to the video rental section, he fought off feeling like a sleazebag.

Why should he feel this way? He could be here just to rent a regular video. No one could read his mind. Unfortunately, a mother and son were already inside, as they scanned the children's shelf, which was mostly cartoons. Rob-O strolled immediately to *NEW RELEASES*, pretended to study the titles.

After the pair made their selection, left, and he was alone, he made his way over to the *ADULT* section, like only mature people hung out there. He didn't kid himself. He *was* a sleazebag...for being there, for renting something that only made him more self-conscious about his small penis, for being turned on by women giving it up for money. Whoever invented modestly priced VCRs and the concept of video rentals, the sub-concept of X rentals was also a sleazebag. Big time. He hoped to make his selection quickly, pay for it at the front cash register when no one was around. He grabbed a tape with a hand-scribbled title pasted on the front: *GIRL ON GIRL SAFARI*. Then he stood frozen in the porn section of Moody's video rental department, undecided. Was he really going to go through with this?

Finally, first tape in hand, he inched his way towards the farthest corner of the *ADULT* section, a place he had never visited, thankfully dark from bare lighting. But then a young local in his twenties entered the room. Rob-O hustled back to *NEW RELEASES*. He didn't recognize the man, so that was a plus. The guy had on an Adidas track suit and a white floppy bucket hat, and without inhibition made his way over to the dark corner *ADULT* section Rob-O had just vacated. Perhaps he sensed Rob-O was conscious of his presence—or had seen Rob-O in the very same spot—because he casually glanced back towards Rob-O. Then the young man reached into his jacket pocket, took out a red bandana, and stuffed it into the right back pocket of the track pants, most of it hanging out.

Rob-O knew he should leave, be happy he had *GIRL ON GIRL SAFARI*, a tape he held in front of his chest, the title pressed snugly against his tee shirt.

The man took one more look back at Rob-O, whose feet remained glued to the same spot—was that a smile?—then picked out a video and exited.

Rob-O executed a deep exhale. He needed to get this shit over with. He waited a few moments. No one else came in. Rob-O rushed to the dark corner, grabbed the first video within reach, scurried straight to the cash register.

A bag was not offered for video rentals. Most of the VHS *ADULT* tapes were unmarked copies of either an entire X movie or snippets of many. As a veteran video renter, he had brought along his own plain brown bag, pulled from the lower right-side pocket of his cargo shorts. Rob-O couldn't look Moody in the eye when he paid him, so he didn't know for sure if the titles registered with the store owner. But Rob-O knew Moody usually noted what was rented, and probably judged him badly, so he snatched the videos from Moody's hand, stuffed them in the brown bag, hightailed out without his change. Outside, he power-walked to the corner and made the turn towards his car. If someone he knew had seen him come out of Moody's with his personal, full brown bag, they would know for sure that old sleazebag Rob-O had not been there to buy a mango.

The thing he probably missed most about college was that back then he didn't give a fuck. Now, knocking on the door of thirty-seven, he seemed to care about everything. And he mostly cared about what Kate thought. And he mostly dwelled on what would make her happy.

He drove back to the resort, hoped to have enough time to hide the tapes somewhere in the bedroom. If he left them in the car, they would probably melt in the Caribbean heat. He hadn't rented a video in a long time. Didn't need to. He had the very real thing. He also lived with someone else now so there was hardly private space or time or need to rub an extra one out.

He drove his Datsun through the gate, waved at Yankee, motored up the entrance road, halfway around the roundabout, up the bluff road, parked in the driveway of his house. Kate was below prepping for Yoga in the Shade. Rob-O hid the tapes under the bed, drove back down, and parked near the waterfront. He would need the car to bring up the VCR and monitor. Sweat poured out of his body, soaked his Hawaiian shirt and cargo shorts, compounded his stress.

Later, Kate cooked dinner while he unloaded the monitor and deck and set it up in their bedroom. She looked at him quizzically when he brushed by her in the kitchen with the monitor.

"A surprise," he murmured, sheepishly.

"Oh, shit!" Kate blurted as she stirred her meat sauce. "Wednesday."

He had always admired her intuitiveness.

She said nothing during dinner. She knew he liked to surprise her.

Done, she cleared the table, he washed the dishes. They retired to the upstairs master bathroom, threw off their clothes, stepped into the shower stall. This evening ritual of showering together was one of his favorite times. They kissed deeply. Washed each other. Shampooed the other's hair. The warm water that sprayed onto their shoulders and shimmied down their bodies added an extra spark to their kissing.

He was soon erect. She touched him there. More like held him.

"Let's do it here," Kate said.

"The surprise."

He could sense her disappointment, but she simply kissed him again. There it was, just like he and his buddy had postulated on the sailboat. He knew part of her would like him to give up his quest to please her completely and would prefer no special Wednesdays. (He really had backed off for a while.) But she said nothing. Just kissed him. No problem. Not suddenly something or someone he had to deal with.

They dried each other with beach towels, then he led her to the bedroom. He had already set up the monitor on a chair at the end of the bed, the wire from the back running down to the VCR on the floor. She got into bed. He popped in *GIRL ON GIRL SAFARI*. They laid on their stomachs, propped up on their elbows, faced the TV, feet pressed against the headboard, and watched.

Four women in their twenties wore skimpy animal outfits: leopard spots, zebra stripes, lion mane, tiger stripes. The only other actual safari elements were additional (feeble) attempts at plot: two hid in the bushes while the other two stalked their *prey*; shot outside in a dry, hilly area that looked more like Southern California than Africa. The two stalkers finally captured the ones who hid. And that was when the party (safari?) started. They deserved a blanket to work on, but somehow the director must have thought if all the action took place on grass it would be more realistic.

Kate said, in a perfectly serious tone, "This is a total objectification of some obviously well-intentioned actors."

Rob-O looked at her. She held onto her solemness. He had fucked up.

Then she burst into laughter.

He laughed, too, then whined, "You got me. I thought for a second our relationship was over."

She kissed him deeply, said, "They are hot."

He turned towards the screen. The zebra and tiger, all stripes, grinded and made out.

Kate watched.

"You can touch yourself," Rob-O said.

"It's more wacky than a turn on."

But Rob-O was soon erect. Kate hadn't quite been able to get there when she had watched Alvin and Twiggy going at it. He hoped two women might do the trick.

When the lion fingered the leopard, it took much willpower for Rob-O not to prop Kate up on all fours, enter her from behind so they both could go at it while they faced the action on the monitor, which was now accompanied by intense—TOTALLY FAKE— orgasmic moans. But despite his arousal (two hotties going at it, are you kidding?), he held back. She hadn't put her diaphragm in yet, knowing that special Wednesdays, more often than not, did not involve intercourse.

Nevertheless, he couldn't help but make his way behind her, as he gently slid his hands under her belly, and propped her up. They watched together. He began playing with her nipples, used the two-finger caress technique she enjoyed so much. He heard a moan. Or was that the zebra? Again, he was tempted to enter her. The lion had the leopard on all fours, too! But Wednesdays were about her pleasure.

He would really like to know if he wasted his time, or there was something about the movie she liked. Watching. Four others. While your lover tried to make you feel good.

He slid his right hand down between her legs. There was a moistness, but not as much as Sunday, Monday, Tuesday, Thursday, Friday, and Saturday. He used his index finger to rotate small circles against her clitoris.

They continued to watch, like the dirtiest of voyeurs. Two nearly naked women kissed on the TV screen. The hunter and the hunted explored, grinded, humped with bodies, tongues, fingers, and hands. Rob-O picked up his pace. Kate moaned but did not seem anywhere near the orgasm path he was on, as he took care not to let his penis touch her buttocks or it would all be over for him.

Kate finally flopped on her belly, let out a frustrated groan. He slid his hand away, already a bit cramped.

He jumped off the bed, spanked the VCR's eject button. The tape spit out like a thick black tongue making fun of him.

She exhaled deeply. That was all she would do. She wouldn't complain. She knew he meant well.

But he gathered his courage, picked the other tape off the floor that was next to the VCR. This one did not have a title taped on it. It was a beat up, used tape. Cracks were visible in the clear plastic center. He had no idea if there would be some fake storyline, bogus costumes, or just random scenes. It was his last try. He promised himself there would be no more special Hump Day Wednesdays if this did not work.

He got back on the bed. She laid down on her back with him, their heads now propped up on pillows by the headboard, as they peered between their bare feet at the new movie in front of them.

It was all men. All gay. No pseudo-plot. No special attire. Rented from Moody's *ANTIMAN SECTION* (though there was no sign labeling it). A quick scene of two men having intercourse. Then another with oral sex. Rob-O and Kate watched, silently. She didn't murmur any cute jokes. He was tempted to cover his shrunk penis with a sheet, but that would be too obvious. At the moment he was sure that renting this tape was not worth the headache, or worse, the wrath of recognition by Moody, who knew exactly who Rob-O was and where he worked, and now assumed he was an *antiman*.

As each cut and spliced scene transformed into the next, the screen would go fuzzy with lines then new man-on-man action would start. The third transition included two young men, shirtless, one in boxers, the other in briefs, one with a thick moustache, the other clean shaven. They kissed. They made out. As lovingly as any man and woman Rob-O had ever seen. Rob-O lay perfectly still, avoided a sudden move that could break the abrupt mood change, or a word that would stifle the new flavor in the room started by Kate's soft sigh.

He glanced sideways at Kate, as he had when Alvin continuously pressed his lips on Rob-O's, forced his tongue into Rob-O's mouth against full resistance.

She touched herself.

All the men did was kiss. The more they did, the more they moaned. The more Kate moaned. Their sounds were way more sincere than the safari girls. Kate rubbed her fingers faster between her legs, moans transitioned to a high-pitched, passionate rumble from her throat. An unfamiliar sound, except it did harken back to that night on the beach, under the shadow of the bluff.

Rob-O so wanted to kiss her cheek, encourage her, make out with her, massage her breasts, replace her finger with his, even enter her from behind so she could feel him, yet still have an unobstructed view.

But he held back, clear that, at this moment, she was again the solo fly on the wall, isolated, wanting no one else in her space.

Then her eyes slammed shut, perhaps behind them an ongoing vision of two men whose tongues touched, lips mashed, lost in the throes of a simple passion produced only by kissing. Her body undulated, her head rose with her neck, then back down as the tremble passed through her shoulders, dipped onto her belly, rippled down her torso, onto her legs—as if she wobbled on a giant waterbed—then climaxed with a deep, clenched curl of her toes. And that scream. That scream he had only heard one other time. That scream proclaimed that the carnival bell had tolled once again.

Oh, how Kate did come.

Neither of them gave a flying fuck that her orgasm could be heard at John's house above them, the grand house above that, and perhaps all around the resort rooms, down the road and out through the gate, maybe into Old Hill Village and beyond.

It was a glorious release and Rob-O stared, frozen, took it in, absorbed as much passion as he could from his magnificent lover.

"I love you so very much, Rob-O!" Kate belted at the very end, with that night-under-the-bluff intensity.

Then she collapsed within herself, flung her fatigued hand dramatically off to the side, tried desperately to slow down her gasps and whimpers, until he pulled her into his arms to stop the shaking, their bodies entangled as they kissed, everything still except for the graceful embrace of their tongues.

"Kate, I lo—"

"You don't have to say it," she interrupted breathlessly. "What you must have gone through to rent this video says it all."

TWIGGY & NED

Twiggy reclined in their master bed as close to the right side as possible—while Ned snored like a stallion with a chest cold on the other end—when she heard Kate scream out her love for Rob-O. Though it was not appropriate for the guests to hear, and certainly those in Buildings Three and Four could, Twiggy could not erase her smile. At least someone up on the bluff was getting it and getting it good.

At times like these, she wondered what it would be like to have Alvin next to her instead of Ned, to be in a nice, relaxed, traditional place, like real lovers, without their frantic search for time together, whether in the guest room or some secluded spot around the resort.

What would it be like to truly have Alvin as a partner? What would it be like to be free of the snore and have a man who loved her and whose primary purpose was to make her feel good? Alvin certainly made her feel good. But sex with him was like a flame lit then suddenly blown out as soon as it ended. He certainly did not love her.

And she knew in her heart that Alvin could never be a true lover. He was so focused on the process, on, ultimately, fulfilling his own needs. The pleasure he gave seemed more about personal reward and satisfaction for a job well done, rather than finding joy from the fulfillment of his partner. It was not like he didn't care about her needs. He gave her glorious attention. But it felt as if it could have been anyone, just another female to couple with to get the release he craved. All, possibly, an addiction for him. Doing one type of thing could never be enough. Having only one partner could never be enough. Having a wife and one family could never be enough. She suspected that the variety he craved, whether it was someone else who worked on the property (there was no one she knew about), or someone from Old Hill or anywhere on the island, or yet another wealthy middle-aged guest, husband or not, or some college debutante, all seemed part of craving some new lewd level of satisfaction, a level perhaps immediately attainable but never completely gratifying because of the absence of love and the desire to be on to the next.

Sometimes Twiggy felt that Ned kept Alvin around because, in the utmost discreet way, he kept quite a few guests happy, returning year after year for more. Returning like she did.

Part of her wanted to break away from Alvin, assuage her guilt, live up to the valued teachings of her mother, avoid the angry wrath of Ned if they were discovered. But she had gotten so dependent on the texture of his rough hands and their pressure against her body—whether a caress along her shoulders, a stroke between her legs, a squeeze of her breasts, or a coax of her nipples with his nimble fingers—along with the delight of his long, thick tongue and lips that awakened her needs, made wet oral love to her, inspired the full moist bloom of her passion.

Twiggy closed her eyes and tried to sleep.

Ah, Kate. Good for you.

The next day, Alvin approached her at the gazebo by the west lawn, where she liked to watch the sunset over the water. He did not sit down, far too intimate, and stood a few steps away as he took in the orange of the horizon but spoke directly towards Twiggy.

"I have a new spot on the property, Miss Twiggy. Secluded and safe. Mister Ned and John have an appointment at 8 tonight in his office with the white-haired gentleman who wants to have his shareholders meetin here next fall."

On one hand, Twiggy preferred their clandestine encounters in the guest bedroom of the grand house when Ned was off the property. She was the most relaxed. But their naughty outdoor encounters were among the best. The time on the sand, under the bluff with Ned above them, as he listened to some baseball game on the radio—or had his own wank—made her heart race triple time. If only the tide were more predictable.

Her nod towards Alvin was almost imperceptible.

"Walk the path towards the tennis court at 8:15," he said. "I'll find you."

She had taken her usual late afternoon shower, but wanted another one after dinner, except that might make Ned suspicious, especially since there was no special social event going on that evening. She made time, while locked in the bathroom, to make sure she was extra fresh down there. Her fingers trembled as she grasped the washcloth and rubbed herself clean. If Alvin hadn't scheduled something this evening—so aroused since she heard Kate and fantasized about Alvin—she could've easily finished herself off.

But why indulge in an appetizer when she could have the entire meal? Or at least the entrée (no dessert)? She was in such a state that even if she orgasmed, she would be ready for Alvin. She completed her cleaning, pressed as lightly as she could with the rough surface of the cloth.

She wore a plain white dress to avoid even the chance of Ned's suspicions, but wore her cream-colored, skimpy, bikini-cut, silk panties underneath. Alvin's favorite.

It was already dark. She glided down the bluff road towards the bell at the roundabout, as if on the way to the dining room. Ned had gone down twenty minutes before to prepare for the meeting that was probably just starting. Twiggy saw a few guests stroll the property, so she waited until they slipped out to the beach between Buildings Two and Three. She didn't see any resort staff, so she made the left towards the tennis court path.

The lone, dusty, red clay court was a relic at the resort. Built by a local, non-tennis crew, it was stuck in the corner of the property, hidden from view whether standing at the roundabout or the bay waterfront because of a thicket of trees and bushes, tucked below the backside of the bluff, only visible from a boat out at sea. At the top of the bluff, no one could see the court because you couldn't get close enough to the edge to look straight down. Because of the hot weather, it was rarely used by guests.

"Follow me, Missus," Alvin said as he emerged from the bushes.

He did not take her hand. They were still not as invisible as they could be.

On the far side of the makeshift fence that bordered the court, in an open space surrounded by bushes full of colorful flowers, Alvin had already laid out a blanket on the grass.

His prep work brought a smile to her face. Could he possibly desire her as much as she desired him? The intensity of all they shared, all he did to her, made her feel that somehow he did.

The fact that this location was not completely foolproof, also made this night that much more thrilling, though she never, ever wanted to get caught.

All of it inspired another level of titillation when he held her in his arms and kissed her deeply.

Then he laid her down on the blanket.

"Excuse me, Missus. I'll be right back."

Alvin made his way through an opening in the bushes. There was one overhead spotlight in this area, halfway up a palm tree, which shed direct light down, there to simulate some sense of safety if a guest wandered this way, which rarely happened. Beyond the fence and trees, at the far baseline side of the court, was the bay, where balls shanked by beginners disappeared. Past the side of the court where Twiggy lay, around the bluff edge, was one additional space that housed a small concrete building full of garden tools, and extra potted plants for the property, kept neatly by the head gardener who arrived every morning at sunrise. Closer to there, away from any light, would probably be a safer spot, but if they remained at this location, under the light, it would allow her the luxury to absorb all the details of Alvin's beautiful body.

Beyond the bushes, she heard a heavy tinkle as his stream splashed the dirt.

Her breathing shuttered. If it wasn't so dirty, if it didn't chance ruining the image Alvin had of her as the dainty patron lady of the resort, she would follow him back there. Just to watch.

He returned, laid down beside her, placed a hand on each of her cheeks, brought her face towards his and delivered the most sensuous of kisses.

She melted.

How he got her dress over her head and off, she wasn't sure. It seemed like one quick, effortless motion. He saw her panties.

"So sexy, Missus."

He left them on. Perhaps it seemed naughtier when he worked his finger under the elastic and deep inside her.

Then he was naked, too. And, again, her fullest pleasure was not just from laying back and being pleased by him. She ran her hands over every curve of his chest, along the square packets of abdominal muscles, as if her fingers traced an exhilarating obstacle course.

"You're so beautiful," she whispered.

There was always a choice between eyes closed to stay lost in this fantasy come true, or open so she could take in the full bulk of Alvin's powerful masculinity. She did both. Eyes closed as he fully sucked her delicate nipples, opened as she watched him work his way down her body with licks and kisses. A fine sheen of his back sweat already glistened in the lamplight.

He bypassed her center and continued down her legs, until he propped up on his knees, and his hands grasped her right ankle, pulled her leg up so he could have access to her toes as he massaged the heel of her foot.

He sucked her toes, and she whimpered like a teenager. She kept her eyes open because she also felt great pleasure from his reaction to fulfilling her desires—that magnificent, dark hardness.

Done with her toes, he finally removed her panties, laid them on the grass, then climbed back up her body to kiss her fully on the mouth. His manhood grazed her middle; no it was too firm for a graze. The flesh-to-flesh contact, there, at that spot, felt like a bludgeoning, and she moaned, perhaps a bit too loudly considering where they were, but she could not help herself. She stroked him and he murmured his approval.

And then, for the very first time since their initial encounter, she felt his swollen head press firmly against her opening.

"Ya want it?" he asked.

"Don't!" she cried.

"No worries. I do nuthin ya don't ask for."

But the way he moved his hips made his hardness brush her again, and again, back and forth, lightly now, but with enough pressure so that she felt herself soak and unfold for his penetration.

If they were on the bed, she could resist him. She could speak more firmly. In a room, in her house, she could latch onto the words of her mother and keep this affair, if you could call it that, from reaching too far.

But she was on her back, on a blanket, on the grass, surrounded by tropical flowers and palm trees, as the softness of the water lapped from the bay just yards away, and the feel of him against her inspired a dizzying sense of submission.

She reached for his heavy thickness and guided him towards her opening.

It was he who hesitated by arching his back.

"No, Missus. You must ask."

"Please."

"Please what?"

She thrashed a bit. Turned her head to the side. The ache for this penetration came from somewhere deep inside.

"Do it," she sputtered.

"Do what?"

"Make love to me."

He hesitated.

"Please," she repeated, this time with the softness of a contrite handmaid.

He was inside her for the first time. A noble piercing, wide and with force, but not painful because she was so wet. And she knew, for sure, that at no point would she ask him to stop. She wrapped her arms around his shoulders, crossed her legs around his waist, pulled him deeper.

"Do you have a condom?" she asked.

· "Not with me, Missus. You want me to stop?"

It had been so long. The sensations between her legs were so intense it was as if she suddenly had the private parts of a stranger, no maybe an old friend from somewhere long ago, nothing like this, but appreciated so much more now in her forties after such a long time away.

Probably too old to get pregnant. AIDS? Not on the island yet as far as she knew.

She thrusted up against him and he went deeper. She groaned. Uncontrollably. Alvin, always in control no matter how much passion he felt, kissed her deeply on the mouth to quiet her sounds. The desire nearly choked her as the taste of his tongue elevated every delicious sensation.

She wanted it to last all evening. She could even welcome a break then a re-start. If she was insane. If they weren't in the middle of a resort. If Ned's meeting wasn't about to end. If she wasn't married.

So she made the only sane choice for such insane passion out under the Caribbean night full of bright stars above. She let go. Bucked her hips to meet his thrusts, as she matched his intensity.

Which galloped Alvin even faster, as if she had slapped him on the ass.

She really was crazy. To cheat on her husband. To violate her mother's wisdom. With Alvin. Without a condom.

How could someone have this much force? This much energy? How could he go so deep? How had she done without this for so long?

She came first. Hard. With ferocity.

Then he started to come.

It gave her extra pleasure to hear the deep groans of his orgasm, Alvin normally so quiet when he finished on her belly. To her surprise he withdrew (out of kindness or ritual?), ejaculated as usual on her stomach but saved some this time for her small, coconut-shaped breasts as well. Her petite size barely sagged and hid her true age.

Then it was over. He rolled off, rested beside her. Once again, she could see little difference in the size between Alvin's pre or post orgasm erection, as if one encounter could never be enough. He reached for her panties lying in the grass next to them, held them up under the light for one last look, placed them on a dry spot on her belly.

Then, uncontrollably, without concern for anyone being nearby, drenching and noisy, coupled with gasps and wet rivulets running down her face...she wept.

OCTOBER 8, 1989

Alvin's burial occurred on a Sunday morning at the Old Hill Village Cemetery, located at the end of town in the direction of the airport. Reggie was there, in his standby Sunday best suit, both the jacket and pants snugger than he thought they should be, but he'd had this suit for years. He walked with a small procession, up a hill, past cracked or broken headstones with faded names that went back seventy years or more. The newer headstones were thicker, more upright, some graves with a wire fence surrounding the plot. Six pallbearers, stocky male residents of Old Hill, struggled to keep the plain wood coffin balanced as they lumbered to the site. Twiggy had paid for everything. She could've used the Old Hill Village Fund, but Hugo's aftermath seriously depleted it. She would've used her personal account, if she'd had one. Instead, under the guise of buying new dresses to replace those *supposedly* ruined by the storm, she extracted the necessary sum from Ned. He wouldn't notice she still wore the same old outfits.

Twiggy dressed all in black, along with Becca and Kate. Kate borrowed her dress from Twiggy—after a few alterations in the hem since Twiggy was taller—as Kate had arrived on Antigua with one simple suitcase and no formal clothes. Rob-O had no long pants aside from khakis. John had gotten him a spare dining hall jacket used by patrons who forgot their own. Rob-O kept it buttoned to cover as much of his Hawaiian shirt as possible. John looked tall and elegant in his dark suit.

It surprised no one that Ned wasn't there.

The grave had already been dug and the pallbearers used heavy straps to lower Alvin's unwieldy coffin. The pastor from the local church stepped forward, a small man in a black suit, white shirt, black tie, thick gold-rimmed glasses, a bible pressed against his chest. He spoke eloquently, but briefly, about the eternal heavenly existence on the other side that awaited all non-sinners and those who asked sincerely for God's forgiveness.

Rob-O gave John a wry smile. Neither of them thought of Alvin as a non-sinner, as someone who asked for forgiveness, and certainly not as someone who made it to the eternal heavenly side.

Reggie studied the faces of all who attended. There were nine women, dressed in various outfits in black, between their twenties and forties, accompanied by a similar number of children, ranging in ages from toddlers to teens, with one baby, wrapped in a blue blanket, held close by a young mother with long, straight black hair. Reggie was sure more women would like to have come but did not want to send any red flags to husbands, boyfriends, or neighbors. The children were listless, without emotion. Very few, if any, knew Alvin as a father. Some women cried. Alvin's neighbor Juanita dabbed at her left eye with a white handkerchief. Reggie studied the sad expressions on the faces of Twiggy and Becca. Kate was neutral. John was solemn. Rob-O struggled to stand still and whispered something to Yankee. The security guard was in a decent but worn dark suit, his thick dreads hanging down. He held an index finger up to his lips to shush Rob-O, along with a nod that implied he needed to show more respect.

The pastor finished his remarks. Two local gravediggers used large shovels to cover the coffin with moist dirt scooped from piles adjacent to the grave. First the locals headed back down the hill, followed by the Long Beach Bluff crew. John nodded towards Reggie. The three women kept their heads down. Rob-O needed hurried steps to keep up with Yankee. Reggie noticed the young mother with the baby approach the grave, then extend her arms, pass him over the submerged coffin three times before snuggling the child against her bosom and walking quietly after the others. Reggie knew this Gullah tradition, practiced by some living on Antigua, was to confuse the deceased's spirit and ensure that it did not return to bother the baby.

He walked down the hill with Juanita.

"You know that mudah with the baby?" he asked.

"She from Bolans. I think Alvin her first."

"Does she have a husband, boyfriend, angry fadah or brudah?"

"No husband or boyfriend. But I don't think the family happy."

"Auntie, you really are on the pulse."

"I ask around. Alvin visit too many ports, but he always nice to me."

"Anything else?" Reggie asked.

"You know the old man who own the resort?"

"Ned."

"The mean one." Her voice became barely a whisper. "Before the storm, he was askin around where he could find Hercules."

Reggie's eyes dilated to full moons. He knew Hercules well. He'd arrested him several times for fighting, for suspicion of assault, for suspicion of more than assault. He was a bull of a man, expert with the knife, whether for personal use or for hire, who kept his head shaved clean and buffed into a gleaming black. He was wanted now for questioning because of a cutting at a club—though no local witnesses would identify him, a clueless tourist had given a description—but Hercules had retreated to the mountains, disappeared, could even be off island. If anyone knew his location, the person would not say.

Reggie calmly whispered back to Juanita, "No one will know we had this conversation."

Juanita nodded then pushed her crooked legs faster, so she could exit the cemetery ahead of Reggie.

After a few discreet inquiries in Bolans, a local pointed Reggie towards the residence of the mother with the baby. He discovered her name was Valentina and she lived with her father and brother in a house behind one that faced the main road. He didn't know the family, which meant they were probably law abiding and were not active in St. John's, perhaps not around much during Carnival over the summer, a busy time for Reggie who was always in charge of security.

He knocked on the door that was painted a peeling white and looked as if it had taken a beating from the recent hurricane. Several inches of space separated the bottom of the door and the floor, the wood jagged and warped from flooding.

Valentina answered.

"Afternoon. I'm Detective Reggie." He flashed his badge. "Saw you at Alvin's funeral. Mind if I come in and ask a few questions?"

Immediately flustered, she looked back into the house.

"Anyone else home?" Reggie asked.

"Just the baby. Fadah and brudah workin."

"Where?"

"Hart's Hotel."

"What they do there?"

"Fadah a cook, brudah a waiter."

A pause, as he waited to be invited in.

"What's this about?" she asked.

"I won't be long."

"Bennie sleepin."

"I'll talk quietly," Reggie whispered as he inched his left foot forward into the house.

Valentina moved aside and Reggie entered the living room.

"Your mudah?" he asked.

"Passed."

"I'm sorry."

"So why you here?"

Reggie looked around for a place to sit and Valentina pointed him towards a worn, brown couch, a tiny hole in one armrest. The room was compact, house modest. A small, multi-colored, water-stained area rug lay in the middle of the floor. He sat. She stood. Reggie didn't make an issue. He understood she wanted this to be brief. Bennie slept in a wood crib in the corner of the room. Upon closer look, he appeared to be about five to six months old. A poster was taped to the wall behind him that depicted Whitney Houston in jeans and a white tank top.

"You like Whitney?" Reggie asked, as he tried to relax Valentina.

"You know her?"

"Her name on the poster."

"I see."

Reggie pseudo-sang: "*Oh, I wanna dance with somebody…*"

Valentina couldn't help but giggle. "My favorite song. You not so old."

"How old are you?" Reggie asked.

Slight hesitation. "Eighteen."

"You look younger."

She turned towards Bennie in the crib.

"Alvin the daddy?" he asked. She seemed about to say *no.* "I saw you wavin Bennie over the grave."

She leaned over the crib, kissed Bennie on the forehead, so slightly he did not stir from his nap.

"You're not in trouble," Reggie added.

"Why should I be?"

Her back was to him.

"Just one time," Valentina blurted as she turned towards Reggie, as her stress escaped with her voice. "We end up meetin at Jump Up, August before last, in town, in the streets, dancin, Carnival bands playin everywhere, you know in the back of the trucks. I drinkin. Shouldn't have."

"You don't have to share all the details."

Valentina wiped her eyes.

"Did he know it his?" Reggie asked. She shook her head. "Your fadah and brudah know it's his?"

"I told them it was a stranger. Forced himself. Didn't know the name."

"That what happened?"

"I dunno." She leaned over the crib again, this time picked up Bennie, who continued to sleep, sweetly, thumb in his mouth. "I knew what was happenin. I wasn't really up for it, but he was… *persuasive*."

"You can tell me the truth," Reggie said.

"The truth is I made up a story because my fadah would probably kill him if I gave a name. I remember tellin Alvin he must use the condom. He had one in the wallet. I shoulda run right there."

"So how you get pregnant?"

"He took it off halfway thru."

Reggie exhaled a soft moan of sadness.

"Where were you durin the storm?" he asked.

"Basement of St. Mary's school with the rest of town."

He would verify that.

"Fadah and brudah with you?"

She turned her back to him again, snuggled Bennie closer, barely whispered, "Yes."

"The truth."

"No. But they in St. John's at the Pentecostal Church. For sure. Closer to where they workin that day."

He could verify that as well.

"Why not tell me the truth the first time?"

"Scared, Mistah Reggie. Detective Reggie."

"Reggie fine."

"No one on the island seem to know what happened to Alvin. And now you here."

"Doin my job."

"I had nuthin to do with it. My fadah and brudah don't know it's him. I took a chance at the funeral. But I don't want that man to haunt me or my precious boy."

Reggie stood. "I'm sorry for your troubles, Valentina."

"All I have is Bennie." The baby opened his eyes, saw his mama, nuzzled into her chest. "My beautiful boy."

"You know anyone else at the funeral?"

"No. I've only passed thru Old Hill."

"Anyone who might know your fadah or brudah?"

"I don't think so."

"Your secret safe. Here's my card. Let me know if you need anything."

He handed her his business card. She stuffed it into the pocket of her dress.

"So was it the storm, or Alvin murdahd?" Valentina asked.

"Still tryin to find out."

Reggie knocked on the door of the grand house at the top of the bluff. The receptionist below had told Reggie that Ned was at home. She had asked if she should ring him. Reggie said he would go straight up.

Ned answered the door.

"Good evenin," Reggie said, still in his funeral suit.

"What the fuck?"

"Told you I'd be back if I had more questions."

"Who said you could come up here?"

"Would you like the interview to take place below, near the guests and staff?"

Ned stepped aside so Reggie could enter the house, then quickly closed the door behind him. Reggie followed Ned into the living room. They sat on separate couches, faced each other.

"What's it going to take to stop you from harassing me?" Ned asked. "Do I have to ban you from the property? Speak to the PM?"

"It's official business, sir. If you ban me, there will be a citation and fine from the government."

"So what?"

"I'd still come back if I had more questions."

"I'll tell Yankee not to let you in."

"Then I'd come with soldiers. Don't think it would look good with the guests."

Ned scoffed. Reggie understood Ned did not like any situation he couldn't control. But Reggie didn't push his advantage.

"Gracious of you to invite me in. Won't be long."

"Better not be," Ned mumbled.

"Where's Miss Twiggy?"

"At Old Hill. Why don't you find her there?"

Ned was the only one Reggie wanted to talk to this evening, but he didn't say that. Instead, he glanced around the room, focused on a TV monitor on a table in the corner.

"You have TV here now?" Reggie asked. "That the new cable television they talkin about?"

"There's no cable on Antigua," Ned said. "I figured our chief security guy on the island would know that." Reggie kept up his eye contact. "I'll be damned if TV ever comes to Long Beach Bluff, even if cable comes to Antigua." Reggie turned his head towards the monitor again. "That's a TV for the resort's VCR. Rob-O uses it down at the waterfront to teach. And I think he makes short videos for the guests."

"Why's it here?"

"I borrowed it."

Reggie saw the VCR on a shelf below the top surface of the table.

"Makin your own videos?" Reggie asked.

"Renting."

"Moody's in town. I hear it's a brisk business."

"I wouldn't know. You wouldn't catch me there." Ned looked at his watch. "Sometimes Rob-O picks up a movie for me."

"Twiggy must enjoy seein the latest films."

"Sometimes."

"Didn't see you at Alvin's funeral."

"Busy."

"You and Alvin get along?"

"If we didn't, he wouldn't have been working here."

"Do you know Hercules?" Reggie asked, bluntly, as his eyes zoomed in on Ned's reaction.

The surprise and awkwardness from the question bloomed in Ned's face. He quickly recovered.

"I never met a Hercules."

"I asked if you know him."

"Who's Hercules?"

"Everyone knows Hercules, Mister Ned. Someone so up on the television situation on the island surely woulda heard of Hercules."

"You being impudent?"

Reggie had hit his limit. If it was ten years ago, Reggie would probably have been forcibly removed, or roughed up for exhibiting such sarcasm. Except ten years ago only a White policeman could interview Ned. Now there wasn't even one on the force. Now businesses and the government could only hire locals first for most jobs, before an outside White Man, if a local could do the work.

"Just answer the question," Reggie said firmly.

Ned took a deep breath, seemed to stifle his anger, perhaps nostalgic for the old days. He said, "Never heard of him."

"It got to me that before the storm you were tryin to locate him."

"You calling me a liar?"

"Joggin the memory."

"Time for you to leave."

They both stood.

Reggie nodded politely. "If I can verify you made inquiries, they'll be more questions. Only then they'll be asked at the station."

Before Reggie turned to leave, he noticed the tremble in Ned's hand. Reggie walked slowly towards the front door. Ned couldn't see his smile.

THREE MONTHS
BEFORE THE STORM

BECCA & JOHN

Becca did not regret telling John to run again. He liked being in shape. He liked the challenge of improving his time. He looked forward to competing in the half marathon.

But she wished she hadn't.

Because he was out on a run now and Alvin was there, in her bedroom, while she brushed her teeth in the bathroom. How could she care so much about the presentation she made with her outside when she was so ugly on the inside?

They shared one of the grimiest things imaginable.

Yet the pure masochistic physicality of what they did, the heavy emotional acceptance of the pain, especially from one so large, gave her a gut-wrenching feeling that quivered through her body, far more intense than any orgasm she ever had, all because the act itself, with a person who had zero affection for her, proved her total sense of worthlessness.

She believed that if there was a way she could stop this, cast it off, cleanse herself, there was a chance she and John could make it, get past all of it, have wonderful children and a fulfilling life. She wanted children with him. But not when she felt so worthless.

She exited the bathroom, sat next to Alvin on the bed, still dressed.

"Somethin wrong, Missus?"

It surprised her that he had any sensitivity to her emotions. They rarely talked. They only had a limited amount of time, which suited them both, since neither of them had much to say. John's run was roughly a two-hour slot, which they kept to under sixty minutes of their time, as Alvin always waited ten minutes after John cleared the gate before he discreetly made his way up the bluff road to her house. And he always departed quickly when it was over in case John came back early.

"Do I look like something's wrong?" she asked.

"You rarely sit next to me. You still dressed."

He was right. She usually returned from the teeth brushing, undressed, and lay flat on the bed, on her stomach. Alvin seemed to like foreplay with this side of her only, as if it was something exotic.

She could not offer more than half of herself to him. Better it was this half.

"Do you think John knows?" she asked.

Alvin thought for a second.

"I think that time, what, nine months ago, he may be suspicious. Remember when he hit me up on the walkie all the time, checkin?"

"I remember. I was sure he knew. I wanted to stop. But he kept up his training. And the opportunities kept presenting themselves."

Alvin splashed his smile. "I'm glad they did."

Becca looked at Alvin, those remarkable blue eyes. She had a sense of his satisfaction while he performed the act, and as he climaxed, but no sense of his pleasure, or desire, before or after they did it.

"He couldn't possibly know," Becca said. "He wouldn't stand for it."

Alvin nodded.

She undressed. She turned over on her stomach.

He laid his body out over hers, his hot breath at the back of her neck, as his weight pinned her and his muscular arms enveloped her body, which made her feel small, helpless, unable to fight back or resist.

Not that she wanted to.

Not now.

Not when she felt him against her like this as he rubbed against her buttocks, a pleasure for her to feel him become so erect. That was all it took. The rubbing. They never once kissed. She never touched him with her hands or mouth. From the beginning, he preferred not to touch her breasts, nor did she want him to. He never touched her vagina, nor did she want him to. The only lube he used was his excessive spit. She felt it now. Quick bursts of sound, the tweaks against her opening, that drip down her legs. Repeated. Several times.

She deserved to be spat upon.

Then he raised himself up. She felt the dagger-like pressure of him against her opening.

She was bewildered by how careful he was at this moment, how slow, how delicate. He took his time as he entered her, bit by bit, and let her get used to his thickness.

But once fully inside everything changed. Once he found a rhythm and felt her surrender there, he was a beast.

She whimpered. She cowered under him. She accepted each thrust without resistance. The pain was there. His grunt was impersonal, as if he chopped wood and no one else was around. He pounded her body into the mattress coils, then she sprung back to meet the next blow.

"Heal me!" she wanted to shout.

But he knew what he did. Becca believed he understood her incredible need to accept the full, harsh punishment of what they shared. It gave him great pleasure to fulfill this particular hunger within this particular woman. On the sly. The wife of his immediate supervisor. He must feel so powerful.

He was. Indeed.

When he raised up to get a deeper angle, one she couldn't accommodate when they first started, and grabbed a fistful of her hair in his big, beefy hand, she became just a speck of need underneath him. If he picked her up and threw her against the wall to see if she stuck, she would allow it.

There was nothing she could allow or not allow. It was all his need and desire. One that serviced completely her desire to disappear into a puddle of nothingness. There was no other life, no other concerns, no other pain, no other sadness, no other meaninglessness aside from what happened at this moment.

And she welcomed it. Fully. Completely. In a way. A gift. A chance to escape what gnawed at her consciousness, attached as a weight around her neck, one that bowed her head from the strain and followed her during every conscious moment on the resort property, and all through the night in bed next to John, embedded deeply into her dark dreams of living a life without use.

His orgasm was monumental, groans guttural, from somewhere deep. She imagined that Alvin really needed this. There was something he expressed with this destruction that he could not express with anyone else.

Who else would sacrifice her body for the chance to be momentarily weightless in a life that weighed so heavy?

She believed he could not do without this as well, why he didn't stop, though they both had their suspicions about John.

Then he was done.

He stayed inside her while he recovered, the heavy breathing from his chest a pressure against her back.

She would not allow him to see her cry. She longed for him to make a quick exit so she could rush to the shower and let it go in a place where tears were indistinguishable from bath water.

He withdrew. She could feel the drip of his wetness. As usual, she remained perfectly still. He dressed, without taking time to clean himself in the bathroom, perhaps aware how eager she was for him to leave. Or perhaps just as eager himself.

It was normally a quiet departure once he dressed. No goodbyes. No thank-yous. It was over. Spent. With both of them. They would both need time, that seven days to recover before John's next run.

Except this time he pulled a piece of paper from the pocket of his blue slacks. He held it in front of her eyes as she lay flat against the bed, head turned towards him. He said, "I always want to show you this."

She had to stir. She had to sit up. She grabbed two pillows. One she placed over her lap. The other she clutched against her breasts. She reached for the paper, instantly recognized the Long Beach Bluff stationery.

She also recognized John's handwriting. She read: *Stay away from her! Or there will be consequences!!*

She extended the note back towards Alvin.

"Take it. Please. I don't want this in the house."

Alvin folded it neatly, followed the worn creases which made it the square that easily stowed in his pocket.

He left.

The speed of the sprint she executed to the bathroom would've made John proud. She collapsed to her knees, vomited into the toilet, punished herself further by not holding her hair out of the way.

She turned the shower water on hot, entered the stall, let her tears mix with the spray.

After countless minutes, empty of emotion, all wept out, she sat in the stall, hunched on her sore ass, arms wrapped around her belly, and allowed the unrelenting hot water to sting her nipples like sprays from a fire hose. She eagerly listened for the sounds of John's return home. She wanted nothing more right now than for him to come back, for her to step out of the shower to feel his embrace, to rest her head against his chest, to be rescued from this despair, however briefly, by their deepest moment of intimacy.

She hated John for knowing and not telling her.

She loved John for knowing and not telling her.

She didn't know if she would tell John she had seen his note to Alvin.

She didn't know if she would tell John it was over with Alvin.

She didn't know if she would remain quiet but swear to herself it was over.

She didn't know if she would remain quiet but invite Alvin back next week.

She just wished John was here now. Where was he? For sure she was needier than Twiggy, who didn't need time with Ned, who managed her days so beautifully away from him. For sure she was needier than Kate, who was happier with Rob-O, but still happy alone. She didn't need John to say *I love you* all the time. She needed him to be the same with her healthy as he had been when she was sick. She needed him on Sunday mornings for breakfast on the balcony. She needed his full devotion in order to start a family. She needed more than she was getting.

But did she deserve more than she was getting?

For sure she deserved Alvin.

How else could she continue to feel the deep pain of betrayal, the dark agonizing depths of disloyalty shown to a man who she believed loved her, who she believed she loved as well?

KATE & ROB-O

"That's it, ladies," Kate said. "Breathe in…hold…exhale slowly while you stretch those arms out in front." Kate wore her usual leggings and a simple pink tee; she'd stopped wearing her loose cut-off, short-sleeved sweatshirt. She walked between the six women in various types of workout clothes who had signed up for her Yoga in the Shade class, each on their own mat, on the grass, under the shade of a dozen palm trees, hunched down, chest to quads, as if they prayed. "Keep crawling those fingers forward. Stretch that back….And relax."

In the distance, she saw Rob-O's Datsun enter the gate, ride past the security shack, and motor towards the roundabout.

Wednesday. She knew where he came from, where he was headed. Only now he didn't have to come back to the waterfront for the VCR and monitor. He would get it from Ned's house, who just started using it on the weekends. Rob-O explained it was because Ned had heard what a good time they had on Wednesdays.

"Okay, ladies, that's it for the day. Roll up your mats and put them in the bin. Make sure to hydrate."

"Thanks so much," said a perspired red-haired lady from California, as she got in line for the large jug of ice water, as each participant waited patiently with a paper cup.

When they were done, Kate took her own swig.

It was later in the afternoon when Kate saw Rob-O. She cooled off in the shallow end of the bay. Not too far away, a mom, dad, and son received their first scuba lesson. Rob-O stood knee deep in the water, along with the three family members, each with a scuba tank strapped to their backs, a mask and snorkel propped up on their heads. He showed them how to clean the mask with spit and a rinse. Then how to clear their snorkels. Then how to breathe through the regulator attached to the scuba tank. The father went first, then the others, as each submerged underwater to practice their regulator breathing. Rob-O nodded approvingly, then said something that made them laugh. He was a natural born teacher. She caught his eye from about twenty yards away. He gave a half-wave back. It surprised Kate that he wasn't more enthusiastic.

Probably focused on his lesson.

He hardly ever nurtured a bad mood.

That night Rob-O suggested they eat in the main dining hall. He didn't feel like cooking. She offered to make a meat sauce, but he said the dining hall was fine, which meant he had to wear a jacket and a tie, which he didn't like, even if it had pineapples on it.

He was quiet during dinner as they sat at a corner table. John and Alvin worked the room. Each looked elegant in their jackets and ties, as they stopped at various tables and asked guests how their day went, how dinner tasted. A bus boy allowed a cloth napkin to slip to the floor as he cleared a table. Alvin immediately hustled over to chastise him.

Rob-O frowned as he watched Alvin deliver his lecture, as the boy lowered his chin to his chest, faced his eyes towards his shoes.

"Everything okay?" Kate asked.

"Copacetic."

"Isn't that the mouthwash you use?"

Rob-O nearly spit out his beer. He chuckled heartily.

"It's not that funny," Kate said.

"I know. But it's my sense of humor. I laughed because you made a Rob-O joke."

"You're right."

They laughed together. Kate toasted her wine glass to Rob-O's Red Stripe. He only drank beer from the bottle.

Later, Kate prepared for bed, applied cream to her perpetually sun-weathered hands while Rob-O prepared the VCR, placed in its usual spot, for what had now become a ritual: Gay Movie Night. It was the only day she didn't put her diaphragm in before retiring to the bedroom. It was still the only day she orgasmed.

The tape was in, power on, but he didn't hit PLAY. First was foreplay. And she welcomed this.

He was an excellent kisser, which had surprised her the first time. Nine months ago, she had originally pegged him as a lapper, another guy who jammed his tongue in and swished it about like a dog taking a drink. But his lips were soft, tongue gentle. He always paid superb attention to her breasts. Well, her nipples. They both became instantly erect from the touch of his fingers, the caress of his tongue. She wanted to give some attention to him, stroke what was already displayed, but she accepted his expectation that Wednesdays were for her to enjoy fully and have the release so many others took for granted, especially Rob-O, whose most difficult efforts on Wednesdays involved trying not to orgasm.

When he finished her foot massage, he hit PLAY on the VCR that rested on the chair below the bed like a person with a bird's eye view of their action.

She watched. Rob-O joined her in bed, as they lay side by side, heads propped on pillows, and peered down at the movie. She suspected that this first video segment was a re-creation of the famous beach kissing scene in the old black and white movie *From*

Here to Eternity, with Burt Lancaster and Deborah Kerr. Only it was two men, one blonde, one brunette, in skimpy Speedos as they thrashed around on the sand, switched from top to bottom, as ocean waves crashed on shore and rolled over them. Rob-O seemed more focused on her than the monitor, but she wasn't sure, as she slid a hand between her legs and explored. Her moist right index finger found the right spot and she let out a soft moan. He had learned, for optimal success, not to do more than watch at this point.

Kate knew her movie reference was correct when the pair repeated exact dialogue in between their smooches.

"Nobody ever kissed me the way you do," the blonde said.

"Nobody?" the brunette answered.

"No, nobody."

"Not even once, out of all the men you've been kissed by?"

Kate's rubbing became more rapid.

For the first time since *GIRL ON GIRL SAFARI*, Rob-O pressed his lips against her cheek, lightly, tenderly, while she watched. It felt good.

The pair on the screen squeezed each other tighter, continued to writhe on sand and water, their deep interest in each other clear from the large, protruding bulges in their Speedos.

Rob-O re-massaged her nipples.

Kate increased her tempo so as not to lose the rhythm or the bond between what her hand did and what her eyes absorbed from the screen.

Then, surprisingly, as the male couple stripped down completely, Rob-O guided her onto all fours, her head facing the screen. He got behind her and entered her wetness with great ease. This position allowed him to be inside her while they both maintained an unobstructed view of the TV.

"Keep touching yourself," Rob-O said.

She tried, pleased with his penetration, right hand at her center, left arm supporting her weight, and his, as he thrusted forward.

The men on the screen were in the exact position, doing the exact thing, the blond on the bottom, as the brunette pleasured him with his long, thick erection.

She had to close her eyes. She did not want to watch while Rob-O was inside her. She wanted to feel him. She wanted to absorb her connection with him. Her hand dropped away. Both arms now supported her body. She had been on her way. She had been close. But she was glad it had changed to something they could share. She did not want him to stop.

"Look how big he is," Rob-O murmured, breathless from his repeated thrusts. "Can you feel him inside you?"

"I feel only you, my darling," Kate whispered back to him.

This prompted a different rhythm from Rob-O, one more familiar, one not so intent on plunging in deep, out, then back, with such unneeded emphasis on length. It was simply the tempo of the loving tenderness he usually gave and she loved to receive.

With this trigger pulled, the only move Rob-O could make was full steam ahead. She moaned under him. Not from rising orgasmic pleasure, but from the beautiful feeling of sharing their bodies. Then she felt him come inside her with a joyous splash. Hard. He used every extra thrust for a complete finish. Then he pulled out. Rolled onto his back. She collapsed face first. Their heads were by the footboard, oblivious to the monitor, which now pictured a young man giving an old man a blowjob in a dark alley.

"Fuck!" Rob-O shouted, as he smacked off the VCR. "I'm so sorry."

"About what?"

They both breathed deep for several moments.

"Being so fucking selfish," Rob-O said. "You give yourself to me every night. You deserve this one night for your pleasure. I couldn't stop myself from being part of it, from trying to be the one who pleased you. I didn't plan on coming. I know you have a better chance by yourself."

"You do please me," Kate insisted. "In every way."

Rob-O looked down at his flaccid penis, already at post-shower shrinkage. "Hardly."

They flipped their positions, heads now side by side near the headboard, and rested on pillows.

Another long silence as they stared at the ceiling. She wanted to get her words right.

"I certainly enjoy my abandonment from watching two men while focused on myself. But, like you, I don't like feeling distanced."

"But you deserve at least one night just for you."

"It won't always be perfect."

"Sometimes," Rob-O said, "I think you do Wednesdays more for me than you."

"It's a genuine breakthrough for me. It's an experience I thought I'd never have."

"Do you mean it at the end when you shout, 'I love you, Rob-O!'?"

"I feel it all the time. I say it at climax as a total release of my feelings, as a way of connecting you to this marvelous experience, a way to show you the deep appreciation I feel for you being the one who unlocked my body."

"And your mind."

"And my mind, *bro*," Kate repeated, with a perfect tone mimic.

But he did not laugh. Instead, "Except it's Mr. and Mr. who do the unlocking."

Rob-O rolled onto his side, faced away from her.

"It's all part of the same—"

"I fucked up, Kate. I'm really sorry."

He shut the one lamp, pulled the sheet over his body, stayed turned away from her.

She remained wide awake. "My dad used to tell me that things worked with my mom because he always made sure she never went to sleep angry or sad."

No response.

She added, "You seemed a little out of sorts this afternoon during your scuba lesson."

He turned onto his back. "I'd like to cover up for a generally shitty day when I'm around you, but I guess it's not possible."

"Something happen?"

"Fuck yeah."

She waited patiently. Then, "The video store?"

"Is there anything you don't know about me?"

"We're lovers."

"I go through my usual routine. Enter the store when it's not crowded. Always browse the regular videos until no one's around. Pop the video in a brown bag after paying Moody."

Long pause.

Kate: "So what happened?"

"I turn around. There's Alvin with this big shit-eating grin on his face."

"Oh, fuck."

"*Oh, fuck* is right."

"I say *oh fuck*," continued Kate, "not because I give a shit what Alvin knows or doesn't know, but because I know your reaction."

"A completely *oh fuck* moment." Rob-O turned onto his side, faced her. "I nod, hustle out, but he follows me all the way to my car parked around the block. At the Datsun he asks, 'What you got there, Rob-O?' 'Fuck you!' I tell him. 'I thought so,' he says. 'Thought what?' 'Moody was right.' 'Right about what?' He walks away. Which is good because I was ready to take a swing and he can probably kick my ass. But then he turns around and nails me with, 'I must be a really great kisser.'"

Kate gripped the sheet in her left hand, bunched it so tightly into her fist the knuckles whitened, then muttered, "What an asshole."

More silence.

"Rob-O, you can't—"

"Kate, please." He turned onto his side again, faced the wall, whispered, "I just need to sleep."

She closed her eyes. She would not get much sleep tonight. When she did, she dreamt of what she would do to Alvin.

In the morning, she found Rob-O, sleepy-eyed, as he sat in a tall chair in front of the Formica island in their kitchen and nursed a cup of coffee. She went immediately to the refrigerator, pulled out a green and white box labeled *Krispy Kreme*, dropped it in front of him. Both knew this box was gifted to him last week by a guest who came the same time every year with his family, loved the dive trips led by Rob-O, had found out that the thing Rob-O missed the most from the States was Krispy Kreme donuts, and thus brought a box of seven, cream-filled, chocolate donuts from the store in the guest's hometown.

Kate also had a sweet tooth, and for three days straight each of them had a donut with their morning coffee. That ended four days ago.

Rob-O opened the box, pulled out the remaining donut. The doughy bottom was green with mold.

"Oh, shit," Kate said.

"So this is what you think of me after last night?" Rob-O asked with mock anger.

"I didn't know."

He held the donut up, studied the mold. "I was saving the last one for you."

Kate took the donut, studied the mold. "I was saving the last one for you."

"Holy shit!"

"What?"

"We proved my yacht buddy's theory. We passed the Krispy Kreme test!"

"You lost me."

"We proved that each of us isn't one more person to *deal* with."

"By waiting it out until the donut went moldy?"

"By saving the last donut for the one you love."

He stood up. She stepped forward to embrace him.

They kissed.

Then she whispered into his ear, "All I really care about is the love we make."

Then he whispered into her ear, "Do you want kids?"

NED & TWIGGY

For the longest time, Ned took Sundays off from his masturbation routine. It was good to have one day of rest. Especially at his age. But he had to ask Rob-O what the hell he did with Kate that could make someone normally so quiet, scream with such pleasure?

"Ned," Rob-O said, "I prefer not discussing my personal life."

Ned was about to walk up the bluff after breakfast. Rob-O was on his way to the waterfront. They had met at the roundabout.

"You don't have to be specific, just a little clue."

"Things on a downward trend with you and Twiggy?"

"You could say that."

"All right," Rob-O said. "I'll say one thing. It involved watching a video I rented from Moody's in town."

"Really?"

"Yeah. Now I have to go. Water ski lesson."

Setting that up would be complicated. Let's say he watched an X movie and Twiggy showed up unexpectedly. He'd have to pull his pants up, or on, depends, get to the VCR, turn the power off. He could probably get away with leaving the tape in, then discreetly remove it later. But suppose she was suspicious? She could do a quick check of the VCR and discover the tape right there. He needed time to remove the tape and hide it.

So Sunday mornings would be a better bet. Twiggy attended services at a small church in Old Hill and would be gone a solid two hours.

He could adjust his schedule and take Mondays off.

The next morning Ned ambled down to the waterfront. Rob-O poured gasoline from a stained red container into the boat's gas tank. The resort had its own gas pump next to the warehouse behind the dining room. Kate ran a fitness class. Ned walked to the end of the dock where the boat was anchored.

"Good morning," Rob-O said.

"I'm borrowing the resort's VCR and TV every Saturday night and will keep it through Sunday. You're welcome to it on Monday and through the rest of the week."

"Okay." Rob-O finished filling the tank, but Ned was still there. "Something else?" Rob-O asked.

"Next time you go to Moody's, rent me a regular movie. Maybe Twiggy and I will actually do something together. Either way, need a reason for the VCR."

"Okay."

"But also pick me up one of those X movies. On the low."

"Duuude!"

"I never complained when Kate moved in with you."

"Anything in particular?"

"Sometimes, and this better be between me and you—"

"Of course."

"*Occasionally* on my trips to Miami I stop at an adult theatre. Always felt a bit grimy. Never thought there'd be a day when you could do it all in the comfort of your own home."

"Remember when there were no fax machines?"

"I like the Amateur genre," Ned added. "Real people. Real bodies. Real situations."

"I don't know about *real* situations."

"No fake moans. No fake boobs. Not that I don't like them big. But I like them natural. They're so plastic looking when they're all big and standing up, not moving."

"You can stop there."

"Thanks."

Ned turned and made his way off the dock.

The following Saturday, Rob-O set up the VCR and monitor in the living room of the grand house, gave Ned a quick tutorial, slipped him a tape labeled *AMATEUR HOUR* and a worn copy of *FLASHDANCE*. That night, after Ned and Twiggy got in from the string quartet concert down below, Ned persuaded her to stay up and watch the latter, the former hidden next to *BABES IN PARADISE*.

They both enjoyed *FLASHDANCE*. Twiggy liked the music. Ned suspected the story reminded her of the ice skating dreams she had as a girl. The sexy dancing was a nice warm up for tomorrow.

ON SUNDAY:

When Twiggy left the house the next morning for church, Ned unburied *AMATEUR HOUR* and got himself set up in the living room, which meant he locked the front door from the inside in case housekeeping or some other staff person showed up, popped in the tape, made sure all the power buttons were on. He stayed in his shorts, just unzipped. He hiked up his white polo shirt, settled comfortably on the couch.

The first scene depicted a couple doing it in a closet. No dialogue, but you could hear the sounds of their coupling. It was too dark and the girl was overweight. Rob-O had explained how to use the plastic remote control, which had a black cord extended from it that connected to the VCR.

Something about watching a dirty movie in your own home felt naughtier than all his other self-pleasure methods. As the couple fumbled around in the closet, Ned drifted back to something he had learned from his father (perhaps the only thing?). He remembered his dad said, while ten-year-old Ned watched him shave, "Son, always remember, *everyone* has their *public* life, *private* life, and *secret* life." Ned never knew what his dad's secret life was, but he was sure it had something to do with his mother divorcing the man and taking off.

Ned pressed the button on the remote labeled *FASTFORWARD*.

He smirked as the closet scene sped up into herky-jerky, hyper-speed screwing. Then, by taking his thumb off the button, he settled on a touristy looking couple who somehow managed to do the deed in a hammock tied between two palm trees near a beach.

Ned felt a twitch in his boxers. He was never more sure about the truth of his father's words.

All the lovers? actors? amateurs? had solid black rectangles edited in over their eyes to hide their identities. Ned wasn't sure the filmmaker did this for privacy's sake or maybe to make the viewers believe the couples were, in fact, real amateurs. All the scenes used only one stationary camera, which could've been closer, but it was close enough. The couple in the hammock seemed to really get into each other. The girl had nice breasts. With a not-so-discreet grab and stroke, Ned was on his way.

But he held back. This was the first time he could enjoy an X movie in private, instead of when he sat in a dark, dirty theatre surrounded by perverted men who sat as far away from each other as possible. The floor always seemed sticky as well.

Soon a married man went down on his wife while he had her sit on the kitchen counter. Their dirty talk sounded tinny, with a bit of an echo, the sound seemingly picked up only by the microphone attached to the camera. A black couple had traditional sex in a bed. Then an interracial couple had sex outside, at night.

Ned picked up his pace. It was hard to see this last couple in the dark—one light source coming from somewhere above them, the camera angle from behind, the woman's body often obscured by the man's back, the usual black rectangle over their faces—but the pair certainly enjoyed what they did. You could see the woman stifle her moans as the man went down on her with his mouth, but she couldn't hold back the pleasure that rippled through her body.

Ned stroked faster.

The man pulled back from the oral performance and sucked the girl's toes. Then the man was inside her and they both went at it like rabbits. Ned wanted to time it just right and come with them. He could never do this in the theatre like the others did. He usually stored up his arousal until he returned to his hotel room. Back in the day, an X session in Miami could inspire two tosses in the same night at the hotel. But now he wanted to let loose with the man, finish along with him, feel the intense pleasure of satisfying this very tasty bitch as they claimed her together…those beautiful legs, splayed everywhere, on a blanket, onto the grass, around his…

Ned's timing was perfect. His money shot coupled with the man's as the guy sprayed his lover's stomach and breasts. This orgasm, inspired by such a beautiful woman who surrendered herself to such a hunky man, was bigger than any he ever had with Raven, with the Babes, or while he watched various sized and shaped tourists through the telescope.

The guy rolled off the girl and flopped beside her. There was a lull, then he picked up her panties off the grass, held them to the light, took one last look, placed them on her belly. The scene ended, and quickly cut to the next one, which was backseat car sex, but not before Ned was stunned by the panties.

No fucking way!

Ned took his time as the video continued to run. He went to the bathroom, washed up, used a tissue to clean his stomach, peed, then slowly returned to the couch. He picked up the remote, hit *REWIND*; the hard compression from his right thumb turned his pudgy digit a blotchy red. He took the video all the way back to the beginning of the interracial outdoor night scene and began again: the foreplay, the oral sex, the leg and foot massage, the suck of the toes, the teasing, then the penetration, deep and condomless. Ned noticed there was a slight blur on the right side of the picture that never left, as if something was in front of the camera lens, the tip of a leaf probably if the camera was behind bushes, which it probably was, because he could barely hear any sound, just murmurs when they spoke and echoey moans when the right spot was poked. When the grand finale started, Ned creeped up to the edge of the couch cushion for a closer look. He saw the woman's legs wrap around the man's waist like a giant pretzel, long and slender. No one else had those fucking skating trophy legs except...

When the man held the panties up to the light, Ned pushed the *PAUSE* button, moved inches from the screen, studied the still of the sexy underwear on display. Because of the low light—and the fuzzy paused video lines on the monitor—he could not tell the color, but the bikini cut, the lace pattern on the silk just below the elastic was imprinted on his brain ever since their purchase...and sniffed every Wednesday at lunchtime.

Twiggy.

The video was shot somewhere on the Long Beach Bluff property.

And Ned didn't need another camera angle, or better lighting, or the black rectangle removed from the man's face, to know for sure that her muscular, stud lover was Alvin.

Ned let Rob-O into the house on Monday. Rob-O normally came earlier, but Ned had told Rob-O at breakfast to come by later in the morning, when Twiggy usually sat in on Kate's Monday aerobics class.

Rob-O went straight to the VCR and monitor to unplug everything, roll up the cords, and load it into his car to take back to the waterfront.

But Ned stopped him with, "Have a seat."

Rob-O sat on the couch, looked curiously at his boss.

"You ever rent an amateur video before?" Ned asked.

"No."

"Not what you usually go in for?"

"Not really."

"What *do* you like?"

Rob-O seemed to twitch a little on the couch. "Uh, different stuff."

"You ever see anyone familiar in the X videos?"

"What? No. Ned, what the fuck?"

"Where do you keep the camera you use to make videos for the tourists?"

"At the waterfront."

"Locked up?"

"In the storage closet."

"Who else has the key?"

"Yankee."

"Anyone else?"

"John.

"Anyone else?"

"Alvin."

"Bingo."

"Yo, Ned, dude." Rob-O stood. Then sat back down, nervously pressed his palms together.

"Let me show you something." Ned approached the VCR.

But before Ned could turn it on, Rob-O said, "That's okay. I don't need to see it."

Ned sat next to Rob-O on the couch. Rob-O inched away. Ned said, "I think one scene in *AMATEUR HOUR* was shot on the property."

Rob-O bolted up. Walked over to the VCR.

"You recognized someone?" Rob-O asked.

"It's difficult because black rectangles cover the eyes."

"So you recognized a resort location, like on the beach, or maybe by the bluff?" Rob-O plugged the VCR back in, ejected *AMATEUR HOUR*, studied the tape carefully.

"I couldn't tell where it was."

Rob-O put the tape on top of the VCR, sat back on the couch, a safe distance from Ned.

"Why are you so nervous?" Ned asked.

"It's alarming. I don't know where this is going, like maybe you saw something out of the ordinary."

"I saw Twiggy and Alvin."

"Ned, I—"

"Having sex."

"Just them?" Rob-O's voice rose.

"Yes."

"Oh, my," Rob-O exhaled, unable to hide the relief in his tone.

"Not sure where it was. Maybe over by the nursery. But it was him. And it was her."

"How can you be so sure?"

"Let's just say an item of clothing."

"That sucks."

"Then why do you look so relieved?" Ned asked.

"No, it sucks. Big time. I'm just glad you got to the point. But it still sucks."

They sat quietly for a moment. Ned's face twisted with annoyance. He didn't know which was worse: his wife cheating on him with someone who worked at the resort, or that their coupling had been videotaped and seen by who knew how many?

"You should fire his ass," Rob-O said. "I never liked him. I know he's valuable, like when a guest gets robbed, or a tough guy on the staff gets out of line, but—"

"Too easy. How does this stop him from seeing Twiggy? Who knows where, when, how often? No wonder she goes into Old Hill all the time."

"What if you talk to her?"

"Not going to happen. I don't want to deal with this shit. I just want it to stop."

Ned punched the couch cushion, hard, then repeated the blows several times. Rob-O picked up a magazine from the table, waved it in front of his face to cool down.

"Have you ever heard of a local named Hercules?" Ned asked.

"Is that guy for real?" He put the magazine down. "I've heard stories."

"I'd like to get hold of him."

"Yankee would know."

"I need to be discreet. You're the only one I trust with this information."

"Why me?"

"Because you're dumb enough not to say anything."

"That's cold, bro'."

"Don't bro' me till you know me."

Rob-O smirked. "You just make that up?"

"Saw it on a tee shirt."

"I'm sure if you make some discreet inquiries in Old Hill someone will steer you in the right direction."

"Will you do that for me?" Ned asked.

Rob-O stood up to leave. "I'm not that dumb." He packed up the electronics.

"Hey, Rob-O, relax. Just want Alvin to get the right message. Then maybe I'll fire his ass."

Rob-O stacked the VCR and the tape on top of the monitor.

"That tape's not going anywhere," Ned said. "I don't want anyone else seeing it."

Rob-O put the tape on the table, noticed *FLASHDANCE* on

the floor, picked it up. "I'll tell Moody you're buying the amateur tape," he said. "I'll pay for it."

"He sells tapes too?" Ned asked.

"Yeah. And probably pays the amateurs for their footage."

"Son of a bitch."

With a deep knee bend, Rob-O lifted all the electronics, balanced *FLASHDANCE* so it didn't fall, and headed towards the door. Ned followed to open it but didn't. They both stood by the exit while Rob-O strained to hold the equipment and Ned glared deep into his employee's eyes.

"Well, uh, there's this old lady Juanita," Rob-O stammered. "She sells homemade trinkets and bracelets down at the bay. She knows everyone and everything on the island."

"I don't want anyone on the resort property to see me talking to her."

"Go see her in town."

"Where does she live?" asked Ned.

"Next door to Alvin."

"I'll try Yankee first."

As simple as this conversation might seem, Ned didn't know how to approach Yankee. It wasn't that they didn't talk, but when they did it usually meant Ned gave an order or asked a sharp question about the resort. Ned was sure Yankee didn't like him. Why should he? Ned had always kept it strictly business. He treated Yankee no differently than any of the others who worked here. At least the locals who worked here. Sure, he had a more cordial relationship with John, and Rob-O, even the visiting tennis pro, a guy as blond as they come. And yes, Ned understood why Yankee didn't like him. It was just the way of the island, at least at the resorts, at least with him, the same with his father when he was alive.

But just a few days after the video exchange with Rob-O, Ned made his way down the exit road, towards the front gate. It was a midday quiet time and Yankee wasn't in the security shed. Ned looked towards the pool, in case Yankee was talking to the lifeguard, a local. Then he scanned the beach and saw Yankee walk with his arm around a woman who was clearly pregnant, who Ned presumed was his wife.

He hurried towards the couple, waved his arm, a big smile on his face. This was perfect.

"Yankee, Yankee," Ned said as he approached.

The pair stopped, both confused by Ned's cordial tone.

Ned strolled right up to them.

"Wow, your wife's pregnant. I just wanted to congratulate you."

A moment of panic swept over Ned. Suppose this wasn't Yankee's wife? Ned should know if it was his wife. The last couple of years John insisted on a party for all the resort staff, and he invited spouses. Didn't Yankee's wife work in the laundry room? Ned should know.

"Thank you, sir," Yankee said.

"How many is that now?" Ned asked, relieved.

Yankee's wife stared out at the bay. She was petite, hair braided into dreads like Yankee, only shorter, a very dark complexion, belly protruding like a beach ball, their eyes a matching deep brown.

"The baby will be numbah five," Yankee answered. "We have two boys, eight and ten, livin with us. And two older boys, nineteen and twenty, out on their own."

"Hoping for a girl?" Ned asked the wife.

She was too flustered to answer, seemingly bewildered he spoke to her for the very first time. Yankee jumped in with, "We hope so, sir."

"Twiggy and I always wanted children. Just wasn't in the cards."

There was an awkward pause. Yankee and his wife clearly wanted to continue with their visit, but Ned had more to say.

"Uh, Yankee, can I steal you away for a second?"

Yankee looked at his wife. She nodded. He kissed her. Then she walked towards the security shed.

When she was at a safe distance, Ned said, "Yankee, let me get straight to the point. Do you know how to get in touch with a guy named Hercules?"

Yankee seemed shocked.

"What you want with Hercules?"

"I need his help to take care of some personal business."

"What kinda bizness?"

"*Personal.*" Ned tried to stifle the annoyance in his tone.

"His help not the kind you need."

"Oh, I think it is."

The two men studied each other.

"Maybe you ought to ask Alvin," Yankee said. "He know everybody."

Ned let out a nervous cough. Was Yankee fishing? The security guard liked to keep things simple, but Ned knew he was a smart one, why he managed to stay on so many years at Long Beach Bluff. Maybe he already knew? Ned's face shaded red. Maybe everyone at the resort knew about Twiggy and Alvin but Ned? He had to get this nipped before it got completely out of hand.

"There will be a nice bonus in it for you, Yankee. If you can tell me how to find Hercules or get in touch."

Yankee did something he had never done with Ned before. He walked away, towards the security shed where his wife waited, even though the conversation was not done.

Yankee's words flowed back to Ned against the breeze that came off the bay.

"I no involved in bizness with Hercules." A few more steps, then Yankee added, loud enough so Ned could hear: "Alvin mi friend."

OCTOBER 10, 1989

Reggie confirmed with the Pentecostal priest that Valentina's father and brother were at the church during the storm, and a friend from Bolans remembered seeing Valentina in St. Mary's School's basement at the same time. Valentina didn't have the vindictiveness or the size or strength, unless it was a complete surprise, to do in Alvin, then rush to St. Mary's. The father and brother had a small window of possibility, but then they would have gone to St. Mary's in Bolans before the storm hit, which was closer to Long Beach Bluff than the church in St. John's. Reggie knew he needed to get to the heart of what was going on at the resort with Alvin and all the couples who lived there. His best source would be the security guard, the man ideally situated to take in all the comings and goings. Which is why he knocked on Yankee's front door in Old Hill Village during the early afternoon.

The house was concrete, painted a bright yellow, and had a small garden at the front, probably kept by the wife, but ruined by the storm. Yankee answered the door and was surprised to see Reggie.

"Wassup, brudah?" Yankee asked.

"Sorry to bother you on your time off."

"No problem."

Yankee stepped aside and Reggie entered. The living room was neat and had quality furniture. Yankee had done well to keep a job at Long Beach Bluff for so long, though he was probably still underpaid.

Yankee pointed to a plush, oversized easy chair for Reggie, then sat on a maroon couch.

Yankee's wife walked in. Reggie stood, made a polite bow of the head. "Afternoon, Olive. Sorry to disturb."

"Would you like somethin to drink?"

He sat back down. "I'm fine." Then, as he noticed her flat stomach, added, "So you finally had the baby. Congratulations!"

"First girl."

"She in the back?" He stood, took a half step towards the rear part of the house.

"Sleepin," said Yankee. "Girls don't seem to go down as easy as boys."

"True."

Reggie sat. Olive went to the back.

"So, Reggie," Yankee said. "I know you not here just to pay respects to the new baby."

"Yankee, I'm still on the case. With Alvin, you know. I need to ask a few questions. If anyone has the eyes and ears on Long Beach Bluff is you."

"Even with the hat down low over the eyes so no one know mi nappin."

They laughed.

Reggie asked, "Did you know that Alvin was lyin down with John's wife Becca?"

"Surprised you know."

"John knew."

Yankee leaned forward. "That I didn't know." He sat back. "Far as I know, Alvin sneak up there when John go for his runs. Shoot me a wink. But him not smart slippin it to the manager's wife."

"Do you—"

"Not my bizness. I last so long at the resort cause I stay out of bizness that not mine."

"Do you think John the kind to take revenge?"

Yankee thought carefully. "Don't see him as a violent one. Him always good to me and the others." Yankee stood up, walked to the adjoining kitchen, and poured each of them a small glass of Cavalier rum. He returned, handed Reggie his glass. "But you never know when another man try to take what's not his." He shot back the glass, swallowed most of the brown liquid. Reggie put his glass on the table.

"What about Rob-O?" Reggie asked.

"Him more unpredictable. But he have a good heart. Like John. He a funny White Man."

"Did he go good with Alvin? He uncomfortable talkin bout him."

"Don't know what went down tween those two the past year," Yankee said.

"So they used to get along, now no more?"

Yankee nodded.

"Did they ever fight?"

"Now you know no man ever win the fight with Alvin." Yankee took the last sip of rum. "Unless it's me."

The pair laughed again.

"Rob-O a bit scared of the man," Yankee continued. "Alvin liked that."

"What about Kate?"

"She can't stand him. She stopped talkin to Alvin completely."

"Why that?"

"Probably hates the way he treat Rob-O. She love the man."

"Know anything bout the broken bottle I found on the beach near the body?" Reggie asked.

"Alvin a bit of a bully you know. He had somethin on Rob-O. Don't know what. But he like mockin that boy. Didn't take much to get Rob-O from happy to angry face when Alvin around."

"So what happened?"

"Alvin threatened him once. No maybe Rob-O challenge him. Maybe Rob-O just tired of it all. I was at the bay. The bar closed until after dinner. I heard the rum bottle break and saw it in Rob-O's hand."

"And...?"

"Alvin just laughed. Walked away. Hear him say, 'ya one funny White Man.'"

"That it?"

Yankee nodded. "Don't know how the bottle wash up next to Alvin. If it the same bottle. Rob-O have courage. He stand up to a man he know could take him down. But him no kill someone cause he a bully."

"That leaves Ned."

"Between you and me I got nuthin nice to say bout that man."

"Do you know why Ned would have somethin against Alvin?" Reggie studied Yankee closely as he asked the question. No change of expression. Not even a blink.

"Nope. Alvin do his job. Nobody steal anymore or they have to deal with Alvin. The gyals love him much."

"Too much."

"For sure Alvin is one brudah, more than anyone on the island, and that sayin a lot cause you know how it is round here, who don't know how to keep the big bamboo in the pants."

"Amen to that."

They chuckled together.

There was a long pause. Finally, Reggie asked, "You think Alvin lyin down with Twiggy?"

Yankee took a deep breath. "You know Twiggy my favorite White Person on the island. That woman has a heart a gold. Done more around this village than the PM. I just can't imagine."

"Then why Ned askin bout Hercules?"

"I wouldn't know."

Reggie looked around the room one more time, then stood. "Thank you for your time. And information."

"Sorry I couldn't help more."

"You help me. It's a complicated case."

Reggie was on his way to the door when Yankee asked, "Ever think a woman might've done Alvin in?"

Reggie commandeered a convertible jeep from the Army Defence Force in St. George. He was in it now, as he drove past Long Beach Bluff resort, through Old Hill Village. When he got to Cades Bay he turned left just before a large pineapple plantation, drove inland on a dirt road, which was narrow and bumpy, and headed straight up. Large branches lay strewn on both sides of the road. Trees, broken in half, had been turned into mere stumps by Hugo's wrath. With his own car he would have to park at the bottom and do the rest on foot. He was in no condition to hike the considerable distance up, though he had dug out his worn, formerly white trainers. He drove towards Boggy Peak, in the Shekerley Mountains of Antigua, the highest point on the island.

Born and raised in a shanty village on the other side of Antigua, Reggie was well-versed in how to get the word out, to anyone, anywhere. He had it passed on that he would like to meet with Hercules, with a promise to come alone, unarmed, a visit without questions about the stabbing at the dance club near the airport. The poor soul who got cut, and lived, was from another island, Guadeloupe, and had never heard of Hercules, his reputation, his skill with the knife, a switchblade that could appear instantly from his back pocket. And the man was probably too drunk to realize that if someone the size of Hercules bumped into him on the dance floor, you simply let it go, even offer a friendly smile or wave, but never grab such a man by the arm.

If Hercules was wanted for something bigger, Reggie could ask the Army Defence Force to come up to this secluded part of Boggy Peak, but even the Army would have second thoughts. Hercules had a loyal and violent crew spread throughout the mountain (and the villages of Antigua) that made certain parts of this elevated rainforest off limits to everyone else.

The Jeep bumped and crawled its way along the dirt path, surrounded by a heavy canopy of leaves. Extended branches often bumped the windshield and forced him to duck. Finally, Reggie came to a locked metal gate across the road and could drive no further. He had been instructed to shut off the engine and wait.

Out of the trees came two men. One wore a dirty red vest over his bare chest, and long khaki shorts that were haphazardly cut down from long pants; scattered threads extended from the hem. The other wore Army fatigues, the shirt and pants a camouflage of green and brown that blended him into the background. Both wore heavy black boots and carried long, sharp machetes.

They immediately put Reggie through a full body frisk, then covered his head and face with a small burlap sack. Encased in darkness, guided by the elbow along a rough path into the forest, Reggie perspired profusely, from early fatigue common for an out-of-shape, heavyset man on such a hot day, from the typical edgy feeling anyone would have who was about to be in the presence of the Big Man.

The fact they were cousins, not sure how many times removed, but shared a connection to the same distant uncle, helped relieve some of Reggie's anxiety. Just a bit.

As Reggie trudged blindly between the two men, he remembered learning about the history of Boggy Peak in grade school. The name itself came from the sugarcane masters telling their slaves—as a deterrent to them escaping and hiding in the mountains—that a Boogie Man lived high on the peak and would steal their spirits away forever.

There was indeed a Boogie Man. His name was Hercules.

The two men guided Reggie to an open area, onto a splintery bench, where he sat. They removed the sack. His face dripped. The bright sun made its way through this clearing and blinded his eyes after the dark of the sack. Through the light, he could make out a large wooden house with a sagging roof that somehow survived storms with the help of the surrounding forest. Like its owner.

From inside, down the creaky steps, sauntered Hercules.

It had been a long time since Reggie had seen the man, and he seemed even bigger than he remembered. He had definitely put on weight, still broad-shouldered, but burlier. His bald head was as shiny and black as ever.

Hercules formed a huge smile, motioned to his men, who retreated to the steps of the house, then he said, "Yo, Reggie, look like you the one under arrest."

His two cronies laughed heartily.

Reggie looked at the wooden barrel in the shade, cut in half, full of water, a ladle hanging from its side. Hercules nodded. Reggie went over, poured the cool water over his head, then took a long sip after his second dip of the ladle.

He sat back down, studied his distant cousin, who now sat at the other end of the bench. Hercules was always a smart and careful person. Anyone would know that Reggie would not take advantage of this opportunity to bring Hercules in for questioning, nor would he return with more help, if he knew what was good for himself and the health of his family. Yet Hercules had still covered his eyes.

"You say you got no questions about the man from Guadeloupe, so what brings you?"

"Workin on solvin the death of Alvin, the assistant manager at Long Beach Bluff. Him die sometime around when Hugo hit. Could be accident. Could be murda."

"I have no quarrel with Alvin."

"But you're known to provide certain services."

Hercules grinned. Even his teeth were big. "If we're at the station I say it's a false rumah. But since you're up here, alone, unarmed, I can only say that a man has to pay his bills."

The two laughed on the steps. Reggie was glad he could be such amusement. Perhaps they would go easier with him on the walk back.

"So did the resort owner, Ned, try to make contact with you?" Reggie asked.

Hercules smiled again. He looked at his crew. They smirked back. "Me like to keep the life simple. Stay outta bizness that not mine. Maybe cause I'm in the good mood. Maybe cause you a cousin I haven't removed yet." The boys were all nods and grins. "I can tell you that it got to me from someone in Old Hill that the old White Man was lookin for me."

"You meet him?"

"Hell no. I don't spend time in the company of no White Man. If I do, it's a bad day. For him."

"So you had no contact with him?"

"Didn't say that, Reggie. I go into Old Hill and we speak on the phone."

Reggie leaned forward. "What he ask?"

"Offered $1,000 U.S. if I rough up Alvin and warn him to never lay a hand on the wife."

"Twiggy."

"That her name?"

"Doesn't matter. Did you agree?"

"Yes."

Reggie's head spun. He couldn't arrest Hercules under these circumstances. He couldn't arrest Ned without Hercules to testify. And that would never happen.

"So what you do?" Reggie asked as he fought to retain the calm in his voice. "When you do it?"

"I don't do nuthin. Cept arrange to get the thousand."

"So you took the money, but did nuthin?"

Hercules pressed his wrists together as if handcuffed, and said, in a mock high-pitched voice, "Oh, arrest me, Detective Reggie, I took the White Man's money!" The laughter from the steps swelled loud and deep. In his regular voice: "Like I said, *gotta pay the bills.*"

The two henchmen collapsed against each other in hysterics and nearly stumbled off the steps.

Hercules must have taken pity on Reggie's bewildered state, so he added, "I don't mind takin the White Man's money, just like they took our blood. But no way I help one of them, even if Alvin lie with too many men's wives."

"And sistahs," chuckled the man in the red vest.

"And daughtahs," added Mr. Camouflage as he wiped his eyes.

"So then how Alvin die?" Reggie asked, in a simple, flat tone.

Hercules stood, went over to the water barrel, took a long drink, then spilled a ladle-full of water over his head as the drops sparkled against his shiny scalp.

"That's for you to figgah out, Reggie. That's how you pay your bills!"

If Hercules could have filled an arena with sidekicks like his 2 live crew, he could pay his bills many times over as a comedian. This time they guffawed so hard they fell off the steps. Hercules motioned to them, and they staggered towards Reggie.

Reggie knew it was time to go. He stood.

The one in fatigues grabbed the burlap sack, but Hercules stopped him with his eyes. "I trust this one. We blood."

"Thanks for meetin me," Reggie said.

Hercules nodded. The two men led Reggie towards the path.

Just before all three ducked into the woods, Hercules called out, "Alvin dyin was no accident."

TWO MONTHS
AFTER THE STORM

TWIGGY & NED // NED & TWIGGY

Twiggy watched Ned prepare the VCR for what had become their Saturday night ritual: watching a movie together. It was about the only thing they shared, aside from resort business and sleeping in the same bed. In a way, she looked forward to these nights. She had always liked movies. There was a place near St. John's that showed films outdoors, on a decent sized screen, the audience seated on benches or chairs. A lot of the locals yelled or talked back to the characters on the screen and Ned was never comfortable there.

Monitor and VCR on, Ned popped in a tape.

"It's called *THE STING*," he said. "I think it won Best Picture in the early 70s."

"I remember it. With Robert Redford and Paul Newman. I always wanted to see it."

"I did something right," Ned mouthed.

She always hoped for at least one night without sarcasm.

He sat near her on the couch as they watched, laughed together at the funny scenes, both quickly absorbed with the plot.

Ned actually seemed to be in a good mood. The resort was regaining full function—most rooms repainted and repaired, new glass in the boutique window, fresh palm trees brought in, beach back to white sand, old tree stumps and ruined vegetation removed, gardens replanted, pool thoroughly cleaned, dock repaired, beach bar roof rebuilt. Even the tennis court was open and the visiting pro was due to arrive just before Christmas. The phone lines were at full capacity, the airport completely functional. Guests would arrive soon. Some hotels had already opened without being fully prepared, their grounds sloppy, rooms in need of repair, not all the broken glass replaced, beaches still a clump of brown mud. But Ned was a perfectionist with his resort, a trait he inherited from his father. Twiggy always respected that about her husband, that there were no compromises, no holding back on expenditures when it came to maintaining the five star quality of Long Beach Bluff.

Midway through the movie, Ned grabbed the plastic remote, blindly pressed *PAUSE*, then stood and said, "I'll make us some popcorn."

"You're quite the whiz with the remote."

Ned half-smiled. If Twiggy only knew.

In the kitchen, he placed a tin of Jiffy Pop onto the stove's lit gas burner. He grabbed the metal handle and slid the pan back and forth, as kernels expanded with sharp pops, until the metallic covering swelled high into a puffy aluminum balloon. He turned off the gas, placed the Jiffy Pop on a cool burner, split the bubble with the prick of a fork, watched the smoke pour out. He dumped the cooked popcorn into a large bowl, threw on slabs of butter, which melted quickly from the intense heat, sprinkled salt, mixed it all up, brought it into the living room, placed the bowl on the table in front of them, hit *PLAY* on the remote.

"Thank you," Twiggy said.

Ned always liked that about Twiggy. Very polite. Grateful for even the smallest niceties.

They munched popcorn, watched the pivotal poker game scene on the TV.

Ned glanced sideways at his wife. He knew she was a good soul who deserved a lot better than him, who deserved more pleasure in life. Something he could not give. But why did she have to pick Alvin?

His amateur video discovery still haunted him. He could not wrap his mind around the concept of Twiggy and Alvin. He was not sure which was worse:

That his wife had sex with Alvin, someone who worked at the resort.

Or that others might know.

Others might know the true embarrassment for Ned who had become the supreme cuckold. And not only could staff know, but how many on Antigua saw the fucking videotape?

Ned kept the tape hidden with *BABES IN PARADISE.* No one else would see this shit. But him.

At least now, since the death of Alvin, another tape exactly like this one could not be made.

That was probably what helped Ned keep the discovery under wraps. He fumed and floundered for months over it, even came back early one morning hoping to catch them. But now he worried no more. The Alvin problem was no more. Now the only important thing was, *where do we go from here?*

Would Twiggy find someone else?

He could not tolerate this.

Yet he could not fathom a divorce. In many ways their marriage was a sham. Without a child to connect them. Without passion to connect them. What was left?

A partnership.

A bickering partnership.

Yes. They ran this resort together. As a couple. Ned was not nearly as smooth with small talk when new couples or families arrived or congregated in the dining room. Twiggy made everyone feel comfortable and at home. She brought a humanity that made many guests return year after year. Twiggy was probably why the female staff never quit. And now, Long Beach Bluff was not only one of the top resorts on the island, it had become one of the most desirable places to work. There was a waiting list for locals seeking employment.

And the Old Hill Village Fund. Genius. Ned knew she created it out of true, altruistic desire, but the framed poster that described its work and hung in the lobby was read by almost all the guests, many who contributed before they departed, as if it soothed their guilt for visiting a place that retained some qualities of plantation life. There would probably be more hardcore separation between resort hierarchy and staff if it was just Ned, the way it was when his dad ran the place. But all of that had softened as Twiggy advocated for workers and encouraged him to hire fair minded, hardworking John (which Ned would not have predicted, and had opposed), then backed it up with a fund. Genius.

Twiggy was completely absorbed with the movie. He couldn't confront her. He couldn't chance losing her.

Her right arm rested at her side, the hand between them on the couch. In a moment of affection, conjured from the early years when their husband-and-wife relationship was closer to normal, Ned inched his left hand along the couch until it grazed Twiggy's. She didn't flinch, didn't move a muscle. He boldly lifted his left pinky and curled it around her right pinky.

Twiggy let out a quick cough, as her right hand jerked towards her face to cover her mouth. When done, she rested the right hand on her lap.

Did she think he was that fucking stupid? He knew the hand-to-cough move. He had seen it before. Many times. Back in the day. When he came on too fast. When someone really didn't like him. When they were too polite to reject him verbally and went with this ambiguous cold shoulder.

Who was she to be so high and mighty?

She had fucked someone else! While she ignored Ned's needs! And who knew if Alvin was the only one? Ned had remained loyal. He had found his own path to relief without compromising their marriage.

Well almost.

He wouldn't risk his reputation with a personal liaison with Raven.

Never with a guest.

And not even in Miami.

X-rated movies were enough.

Maybe he was just lazy.

No, he was loyal. It was one line he did not want to cross.

Twiggy couldn't tell if Ned caught on to her not-so-subtle cough and move, but she didn't care. The thought of being touched by him was repulsive. And it had gotten worse since the time she had caught him in the guest bathroom. Who knew where and how often that hand was used?

Truth was, she missed Alvin's touch. Her heart ached because of his demise and how it occurred. The only thing she missed more was the sensation of touching him. She regretted the night in the bushes that went too far. He didn't understand why she had broken off their relationship. (Except for the aborted last time before the storm when they thought Ned was downstairs.) But she had to do it. She couldn't go back to what they used to have. But she could not go forward to the place that called her with a longing so deep it had made her cry, and could make her cry, any time she thought about what was missing in her life, and what she had done to soothe a passionless marriage.

There would be only one Alvin. Truth was, there was only one Alvin. Selfish, self-absorbed, narcissistic, someone who marched through life and took what he wanted, when he wanted, without much thought of the consequences. But full of passion that maybe never got completely satisfied.

She knew for sure she would never take another lover as long as she was married to Ned. And she would stay married to Ned. They were married to this existence as the caretakers of the resort. This, ultimately, was the life she had chosen, even after the miscarriage, after the chance to move on while she was still young and able to forge a different path. But she loved it here. Loved every beautiful day she could walk among the flowers, or along the beach, or in town to greet the many true friends she had there. She was essential here. Without her, the resort would revert to what it had been before: a place where mostly White guests were perceived as fully formed, surrounded by workers who were nearly invisible.

She would devote her life to keeping them visible.

She would stay married to the man she shared this with.

She would remain in his house, in his bed.

She would settle for a life without sexual passion—as long as she had the passion of this life.

THE STING soon ended. Ned picked up the remote. He pressed the *REWIND* button, squeezed it hard, as his thumb strained with effort. And not because Rob-O asked him to rewind, which was required for returned videos in order to avoid a fine, but because he was still pissed.

"Never expected that ending," Twiggy said. "They got us with that one. Very clever. No wonder it won the Oscar." She picked up the half-empty popcorn bowl.

"Sit down!" Ned barked. His anger had brewed the whole second half of the movie and he wasn't even sure what had gone on at the end. But now he needed to express himself.

"Do you think I'm a fucking idiot?" he asked.

Twiggy remained standing, thought for a second, as if she wanted to give him a true, quality answer.

"Don't make it worse," Ned added.

"Make what worse?"

"The fake cough. The hand going from the couch to the lap. Do you think I'm that stupid?"

Twiggy paused again, as if she weighed the consequences of truth versus lying. But she did not like to lie. "I'm sorry, Ned. I didn't just want to jerk my hand away for no reason."

"So you were trying to be subtle?"

"I guess."

"You like subtle. You think subtle is above me, something I wouldn't understand."

"If that is the case, I was wrong."

She started her exit again. This time without the bowl.

"I said sit the fuck down!" Ned's face was beet red.

She didn't like his tone. She didn't like his orders. She had some sense of why this overreaction. Rejection. Poor schoolboy Ned. Couldn't handle the least bit of it.

But he was not her boss, and she would not tolerate him talking to her like that. She continued out of the living room, and just as she got to the stairs, about to go up and get ready for bed, he stopped her with, "You'll want to see this."

She turned towards him in the living room. He was at the VCR and ejected the tape. Then he walked towards his office.

"Ned, it's late. I don't want to argue. I have church tomorrow. Early. I stay up with you to watch a movie on Saturday nights. Isn't that enough?"

"So, you do it just for me?" he called from the office. Then he returned with another tape.

"No. I like the movies. I like that we found something we can do together."

"Well then sit down. I think you'll enjoy this tape I came across even more."

She wanted to go to bed, but she didn't want this fight to get bigger. She returned to the couch, sat down, crossed her arms against her chest.

Ned popped in the tape, picked up the remote, hit *PLAY*. He smirked. This tape was cued to just the right spot. It was the only thing he watched on the tape. Repeatedly. Every Sunday. Careful not to view it more than once a week, lest it lose its aura. The orgasms still came, more intense than the others. Twiggy on tape made her other-worldly again, the glamorous model with the long legs and sexy panties, not the makeup-less wife with wrinkles and eye bags who kicked him every night in bed. On the TV monitor, she was once again something he did not possess, but wanted to own. And when he orgasmed along with Alvin, he could project himself as the hard-bodied, well-endowed stud who finally mastered this beautiful creature.

He didn't know which was more intense, the orgasms or the rage the tape produced?

It didn't take Twiggy long to realize what she watched. A part of her brain imagined stifling her moans that echoed from the screen with a wrench of the remote out of Ned's hand that would tug the long cord connected to the VCR which would jerk this evil device onto the floor with a total smash. Or maybe pick up the popcorn bowl and bash it against the TV. Or over Ned's head.

But she just sat there. And cried. As Alvin carefully sucked her toes. Tears had formed instantly. It wasn't the wail that had occurred after the outdoor encounter had ended. Just a wet reflection of the deep pain she felt inside, from the discovery, from the loss, from the emptiness she felt by this unkind betrayal executed by both her husband and lover.

She didn't leave because she deserved this. She had done what he had not. And he had caught her.

Thankfully the video scene ended before her weeping had begun on that blanket behind the bushes.

She wasn't exactly sure why she'd cried so intensely that night. A part of her saw how deeply she needed lovemaking, how long she had gone without it, how important it was to feel this remarkable physical expression of love. Another part of her remembered back to what her mother had said when Twiggy decided to move to Antigua and marry Ned—that Twiggy would know if it was love by the *moment after* lovemaking, that it was easy to get caught up in sexual passion, but when it was over, if love wasn't present there would be a deep emptiness. If love was there, the final embrace, the last kisses, limbs intertwined, or simply lying next to the one you just shared your body with would be the most complete moment of happiness in the world. *Short of giving birth*, she'd added with a smile. Her mother told her that at the beginning of her own marriage, she'd felt it with Twiggy's father, but then, just a few years into it, after Twiggy was born, it was gone. They had continued with an active sex life, but there was always a certain distance, a certain isolation she felt when it was over, as if she was alone in the bed. That was when she suspected he had affairs. That was when she knew the marriage would never be the same. Not long after, there was no sex. Just separation. That night Twiggy gave in to Alvin, to go from such passion to such emptiness—as he held her panties up for one last look—broke her, inside and out, and helped her understand more than ever that she never had that exquisite *moment after* her mother had described. Not with Ned. Not with Alvin. Not with anyone.

Ned shut off the VCR with the remote. She looked at him. He stared at her triumphantly. She was beat. She had no answer. She had no recourse. He did not want her to leave the room. He made her stay. He won. She couldn't go anywhere. Payback for any iota of rejection he might have felt.

He said nothing. Just cracked a sly smile. As if the video said it all.

Yes, she deserved this. But she didn't deserve all of this. She dried her tears with the palm of the right hand she'd tugged away from him, the hand that had inspired this cruelty.

She stood. "Ned, I really need to know the truth. Did you have Alvin killed?"

"I wish," Ned replied. "And that's the truth."

She believed him. He was pompous enough not to lie about it if he had done it.

Twiggy said, "I'm willing to stay married if you are, and continue running the resort as we have all these years. And I promise not to have sexual relations with anyone else, ever again, as long as we're married."

"Thank you," Ned said. "I believe you."

She stood up, walked around the couch, stood behind him. He turned his head and looked up at her curiously.

In a tone still heavy with emotion, she said, "I think there was once potential for something. What, I'm not sure. But I think we had a chance. But it's been too many wrong turns."

She leaned forward, extended her right hand. He flinched, threw up his arms for protection, as if he expected to be struck.

Instead, she grabbed his left hand that had tried to touch her. She gave it a squeeze then planted a quick kiss on the wisps of grey hair still left on his head.

She turned to leave. Stopped. Looked at him with eyes still moist.

"No more movie nights."

Turned again to leave. Added,

"I'll be sleeping in the guest room from now on."

KATE & ROB-O // ROB-O & KATE

Sunday, November 19, 1989 was the date of Rob-O and Kate's wedding. A crowd of thirty or so resort and waterfront staff, who wore their Sunday best, stood on the immaculate green lawn housing the wood gazebo, its framed sides and ceiling decorated with a brilliant flower display of purple, red, yellow, fuchsia, blue, and violet from the various species of bougainvillea, hibiscus, and frangipani found throughout the island.

Away from the crowd, Rob-O stood next to John near the entrance to the wine cellar, his long blond hair tied back neatly into a ponytail, nervous as shit. Earlier that morning, Yankee had offered Rob-O a thick blunt the size of a ballpark frank, but Rob-O had declined, as he wanted to get through this with all of his faculties intact. John, the Best Man, had on a full-blown black tuxedo that included a cummerbund and bowtie. Rob-O had seriously considered going with his favorite cargo shorts and Hawaiian shirt (the one with matching volcanoes on the back). John had begged to differ.

"Why not, bro'?" Rob-O had asked. "There's no fooling Kate now. She knows what she's getting."

"Humor me," John had replied.

He'd fitted Rob-O into a tuxedo as well, with a cummerbund and a compromise that allowed him to wear the pineapple tie.

It was hot and Rob-O sweated profusely in his tux, but was able to maintain a relative calm. On the outside. He couldn't wait to see his beautiful bride. He couldn't wait to be married. It was not a decision he had labored over. It was not something he even thought about much. He knew Kate was the perfect woman for him. He knew that even if he gave it decades of searching, he would find no one better. He had been content with her as his girlfriend. Truthfully, he had never imagined himself in any kind of marriage, whether traditional or non-traditional. But it had dawned on him that day she had worked through his bad mood, the strikeout in the bedroom when he had violated his own rules and orgasmed when she didn't, and had taken on his same anger against Alvin, that Kate was not only a primo girlfriend, but would be a stellar wife and mother. There had been no formal proposal from either of them. Marriage was just something they talked about, and how amazing it would be to live as a couple who someday might have a family as part of their wonderful mix.

The first resort guests, since before the storm, arrived tomorrow, and it would be a return to super-busy. The next break wouldn't be until the summer. They had discussed waiting until then to have a grander ceremony in the States with their families and U.S. friends. But Kate had suggested that sooner would be better than later, and he totally agreed. They would have a second celebration back home with their families in July. But now it was time to be a wife and husband. Officially. Just in time for the delayed new season. Partners in every way. The married couple who ran the waterfront.

Wanting this, agreeing to this, had been the most decisive thing he had ever done in his life.

Kate stood under the flamboyant tree with Twiggy, her Matron of Honor. Kate wore a plain white dress trimmed with lace. Twiggy had given her the dress and helped with the alterations. She looked Kate up and down, straightened the shoulder straps.

"Your body is killer," Twiggy said. "I remember the days when I could shape a dress like that. But I never had your muscle tone."

"And I'll never have your legs."

"It doesn't really matter in the end, does it?" Twiggy added. "Especially with the potential bumps and scars of marriage." She looked out towards the lawn where Ned waited impatiently in his ill-fitting suit. "All that matters is you find true love that lasts."

"I have."

"I'm so happy for you."

Twiggy placed a wreath of yellow orchids on Kate's head.

Kate smiled. She had hoped to find a new life down here, but never expected to discover a soulmate. Rob-O still made her laugh every day. She imagined he always would, even when they were old and barely able to walk. He was the most transparent man she had ever met. From the first day, she could see straight past the cargo pants and Hawaiian shirt to the inside of a man who lived hard, was good at stuff, settled for the simple things in life to make him happy, battled with insecurities, but, ultimately, was at peace. She realized that everything she wanted in a man was right next to her in their bed, and he was the type of person who didn't have to have anything more than what they had now.

It was the perfect recipe for being wife and husband, a mom and dad. She had found a man whose imperfection was perfect.

Lucky, wearing black pants and a white shirt, got the nod from the local judge who would conduct the ceremony and who already stood under the gazebo. Lucky ran down to tell Rob-O, then Kate, that it was time.

The guests were standing in two separate sections that led up from the patio to the gazebo, a pathway of open lawn between them. At the front, to the left of the gazebo, stood Becca. She wore a pale pink dress that covered her shoulders and had long sleeves—on her head the usual, wide-brimmed straw hat—all of it armoring her against the harsh island sun. She had wanted to forego the hat, so unstylish on such a formal occasion, but John had insisted. She liked that he had. On the other side, just to the right of the gazebo, was Ned, red-faced, tie askew, out of place. In the second row of guests, on the left side, stood Yankee and Reggie, both in suits. Reggie was not actually invited, and he tried to stay out of Ned's view while he melded as Yankee's buddy. He wanted to be near the suspicious parties one last time before filing Alvin's case as completely cold.

When Lucky disappeared down by the buildings, Reggie said to Yankee, "Tell me again bout Rob-O and the rum bottle."

"Nothin more to tell. Rob-O don't like Alvin. Alvin like to mock Rob-O. Rob-O break the bottle. Alvin walk away laughin."

"But do you think Alvin make the move on Kate?"

"Sooner or later Alvin make the move on everybody. But Kate love the man she gonna marry. She have no eyes for Alvin."

"Ned my first choice anyway," Reggie declared. "I tracked down Hercules and him say he don't do dirty bizness for Ned. But I have no way a knowin the truth. I do know Ned too much a coward to confront Alvin. But Hercules say it was no accident."

Yankee nodded. "Hercules got a mean streak you know. But him smart."

"I hate to give up."

"You always give it the best shot. Everyone know that."

"Thought maybe related to a gyal in Bolans with a baby, but she no tell anyone Alvin the fadah. And she got too much on the plate to take matters into her own hands."

"Well," Yankee said, as they watched Lucky return. This time he sauntered slowly up the aisle as he carried a small pillow with two simple gold rings. "At least Alvin without troubles now."

Behind Lucky, they watched Rob-O and John, side by side, make their way closer. Reggie whispered, "John got a true heart, but he a passionate man. Passion can make a man do anything."

"You right on that one."

In the distance, behind the male duo, Twiggy walked Kate up from the flamboyant tree.

"No physical evidence. No witnesses. No suspects placed at the scene."

"It's a beautiful day," Yankee said. "Let's enjoy it."

"Yes, time to move on."

Lucky placed the ring pillow on a small white table under the gazebo, next to the judge, then hustled to the side, and, as Rob-O had instructed, hit *PLAY* on a cassette boombox. The rich voice of Jimmy Buffett singing *I HAVE FOUND ME A HOME* washed over the lawn.

As Rob-O strolled between the wall of guests towards the gazebo with John, he whisper-sang the lyrics about how he didn't need anything else because he had found a home.

"You're crazy," said John.

Kate had to laugh as she began her grand entrance onto the grass pathway and heard Rob-O's musical selection. Twiggy smiled.

All eyes were on the bride. John dropped Rob-O off under the gazebo and stepped to the left side next to Becca. As Kate approached, the song ended, and Lucky shut off the cassette player. Rob-O was now breathless anyway, and silent, as he gazed at his beautiful bride, her brown hair done up high, a delicate orchid wreath around her head, a true queen.

She was a queen. His queen. And he hoped he was her king.

Kate stopped next to Rob-O. They both stood side by side under the gazebo, faced the judge, as their hearts beat in the same overtime rhythm. Twiggy moved to the right, near Ned, who was also standing. Rob-O took Kate's hand in his. Instinctively, John did the same with Becca. Ned and Twiggy stood arm's length apart, a clear view of the bay between them.

The crowd settled in, still on their feet.

Twiggy had wanted chairs for everyone, but Ned had insisted it wasn't worth the effort with all the work that needed to be done before the first guests arrived tomorrow.

The judge was as short as he was round. He wore a black vest, white shirt, black pants, and no tie. He had a bushy white beard, brilliant against the coal black of his face.

He said, "Marriage is one of our most important institutions. It is a promise that separates us from other creatures. It is difficult to maintain. It needs kindness as much as it needs love. For when we are kind to each other, we can survive the moments where love might recede. And kindness can always bring love back. We gather to share this joyous day with a man and a woman deeply in love, something they both expressed to me privately, something I see in how each glows in the other's presence. We don't just share the day. We celebrate the couple. And each has prepared their own vows."

Kate unfolded the square of paper she had palmed in her hand. She took a deep breath, but her voice came out steady. She had no problems addressing groups. But it was not her teacher voice that spoke, just her heart.

"Rob-O, I love you dearly. I will dedicate myself to making our union a happy one. You have always tried to understand me and help me. Each person is a mystery and I believe our journey together will be a long and blissful road as we unravel that mystery and find a perfect ending. I came to this place to find a new home. But you have made this a joyful one. I believe we will continue to share much happiness for a very long time. You have defined *love* for me." She looked up from the paper, met the eyes of the judge, focused her gaze on Rob-O, then ad-libbed, "You have defined *kindness* as well."

Rob-O's eyes still had not left Kate since the moment she had walked up the grassy aisle.

She went back to the paper and read one more paragraph, with a bit of twitch in her mouth as she held back a laugh.

"You please me so much with the quality size of your…" A pause. Her eyes did a quick sneak brush down his body. "…heart. And the depth of your penetration to my soul speaks to your wonderful endowments."

Rob-O was about to collapse into a pool of laughter when Kate added with a bright smile, "I promise always to leave the last Krispy Kreme for you."

He held it in. The audience chuckled. He wiped away a tear. Kate refolded her vows.

Rob-O gathered himself. Then reached into his tuxedo pocket, took out his own paper. Unfolded. Read:

"Duudette!" That got an instant laugh from the audience, including the judge. And a smile from Kate. "As you pointed out early on, I'm very good at fixing things. But you taught me that when love exists nothing needs fixing. We are each other. We are imperfect. But we support each other in a way that brings harmony to our imperfections. You have given me the courage to know what's in my heart. You have given me the wisdom to be decisive about life and the future. For this I'll always be grateful. I promise to cook for you. I promise to remain silly. I promise to continue to make you laugh every day. I promise to continue to find new and extraordinary ways to show how much I love you. The future used to be no longer than tomorrow for me. But you have unveiled an entire lifetime before us of love and pleasure. For this I'll always be grateful." Kate wiped away her own tear. "You have the mind of a genius and the *fullness* of a sexy model." She smiled. "And…" He drew the word out, followed by a pause, "…I promise always to save the last Krispy Kreme for you."

The audience laughed. Kate let out a short shriek, leaned over his paper, where he confirmed by pointing to the last line he had written, that it was almost identical to hers.

They embraced and kissed passionately. For this brief moment, alone on their own island.

"Well," the judge said. He nodded towards John and Twiggy, who hustled to grab the rings off the pillow. John gave Rob-O the ring for Kate. Twiggy gave Kate the ring for Rob-O. "We seemed to have jumped the gun a bit, but all is well."

Rob-O placed the simple gold band on Kate's left ring finger.

Kate placed the simple gold band on Rob-O's left ring finger.

The judge finished with, "I now pronounce you husband and wife."

The audience applauded. The spouses kissed again, then turned towards the group, glowing. Rob-O lifted Kate's arm up with his and she followed his lead as they performed a waist deep bow together.

"Indeed, a happy day," Reggie whispered to Yankee, who smiled broadly.

Ned snuck around the back of the group to make sure the food was ready at the dining room, then after the meal everyone needed to get back to work to prepare for the first throng of guests—nearly sold out by the coming weekend—since Hugo had left his mark on Antigua.

The newly married couple held hands as they strolled down the aisle while the resort staff laughed and threw rice at them.

John made a move to follow after Ned, but Becca remained in place and her hand gripped his so tightly he couldn't budge. He looked at her. She kissed him. He kissed her back. Smiled. Then he unraveled his hand and took the back route to the dining hall.

Rob-O and Kate walked all the way down the path until they were alone under the flamboyant tree. New branches were growing back. Limbs full of a brilliant orange canopy of leaves covered them with shade.

Rob-O and Kate gazed at each other as their hands refused to separate.

Kate said softly, "I have a wedding present for you."

"What?" he asked, beaming. "I can't imagine anything that could make this day better."

She looked down at her belly, touched it lightly with her right hand as she let out a deep breath that produced a slight bump.

"I'm pregnant."

BECCA & JOHN // JOHN & BECCA

Just one week after the wedding of Rob-O and Kate, John stretched on the small piece of lawn in front of his house as he prepared for his usual Sunday morning run. It had been an extremely busy seven days with guests checking in, dining room table assignments, resort rooms that needed to become spotless every day, laundry piled high, airport transfers, training Alvin's replacement, the waterfront busy and active with sailboats, windsurfers, scuba divers, water-skiers who dotted the bay like markers in the water. The shallow part of the Atlantic side, where the waves rose then tumbled to shore, had to be marked off again with heavy poles and rope, so swimmers didn't drift too far out, the tide still rougher than usual.

Now, more than ever, he needed his training runs. This one respite, this one bit of time for himself was all wrapped up in this weekly ritual. His times had stumbled after the long layoff during the rocky days when Becca had needed radiation treatments, but he was back on track these last months and expected a record thirteen miles today.

While he stretched, he usually thought about Becca. He always hoped, desperately, that her request for him to train again, those many months ago, was truly because she understood how important this time was for him and not because of her desire to rekindle her fling with Alvin. During the months just before the storm, he often resisted urges to return early from a run. It would be obvious he checked up on her. How could a marriage survive without trust? And if he had caught them together again, there would be no turning back, no recourse other than a solemn, bitter divorce. He very much wanted to remain married to Becca and start a family, like Rob-O and Kate were doing.

On his back, as he stretched his hamstrings, one knee at a time up to his chest, he felt a sadness that would sweep over him periodically because of Alvin's untimely and gruesome demise. Nevertheless, it was a comfort that the threat of Alvin no longer hung over him. There couldn't possibly be someone else at the resort who Becca would choose to replace Alvin. No staff person would have the boldness. Becca was always cordial but professional with guests.

John believed, with all his heart, that there must be a way for Becca and him to build a better, more successful life as husband and wife. He believed now, without Alvin around, they had a better chance.

From the guest bedroom window, behind a shade, Becca peeked out at John as he stretched on the grass. It was during these runs when she missed him the most, especially without Alvin to distract her. She missed her Sunday morning breakfasts with John, out on the terrace, during the months she'd received radiation treatments. She missed John most of the time. He was so focused, so driven to maintain the fluid workings of running a resort—or refurbishing one as he had done these last two months. Hotels, with their rooms to clean, and some services provided, were much easier to manage than a resort, one that all-inclusively fed guests three meals per day, provided water and land activities that not only needed to be well-designed for entertainment and pleasure, but demanded full concentration to remain safe for a population that was generally un-athletic.

Becca remembered back to when John revealed to her the keys to happiness he had read in a book and believed he had found on Antigua: something to do, something to look forward to, love in your life.

Which ones did she have?

Her happiest times had been during their trips to Puerto Rico for her radiation, the way he held her hand, the way she dozed on his shoulder, sure he would not let her head fall, her neck snap. It was when she felt the most valued. It was when she felt secure enough to imagine being the kind of wife who could make a commitment to start a family, who could relish a future with a child, who could share it with a husband she loved.

She thought back to the wedding on the previous Sunday. She was in awe of the devotion Kate and Rob-O had for each other, as if every minute of their lives was for the other. She needed that. She needed to feel that most of John's life was for her, here in this place where she had carved out so little for herself. Selfish? Yes. But she believed this would make her less sad. She had also noticed how wide apart Twiggy and Ned had stood. She could not recall one display of real affection that had ever passed between them.

An icy chill had streaked down her spine as she stood under her hat, beneath the hot Caribbean sun, and wondered once again if she and John were on their way to becoming Twiggy and Ned. The pair's chilled politeness towards one another. Their practiced, superficial warmth when guests were around, who couldn't tell the difference either way. Becca could. Yet Twiggy had clearly figured out a way to survive her disconnection with her husband, to create her own world and thrive in it. Did it make her happy? Becca could not be sure. But she could see that Twiggy looked forward to each day, that she took pride in everything she did on the property and in Old Hill. She'd found a life with meaning.

Yet there were times when Twiggy and she met randomly, maybe paused for a second, stared face to face, while they shared tea, or bumped into each other in the lobby, out on the beach, when they looked at each other with the complete familiarity of studying their own reflection. In the mirror image, they could see the true depths of each other's loneliness.

Becca imagined that if Twiggy had the baby she'd told Becca about on one grey day, that it would have been enough to cure the loneliness, that Twiggy could have built a beautiful emotional life with a child of her own that could include or exclude Ned. Becca felt that life as a mother would be richly fulfilling, would not only give her the additional love she needed, but would strengthen her connection to the man she loved, in a place that provided so few distractions from constant self-examination.

But Becca knew she was not as strong as Twiggy. That woman could do it on her own. Becca would need John every step of the way. She needed to feel the devotion so grandly on display by Rob-O at the gazebo last Sunday, a man who truly *saw* his wife every day, not just during quiet moments on the dance floor, or in the bedroom, a man who put their life together ahead of his personal needs and this breathing thing called Long Beach Bluff. Becca needed this not just when her health was threatened.

These last two months included some very scary moments. Perhaps alone in her bedroom, or out on some desolate spot on the property, even eating in the dining room with everyone else, yet feeling alone. These moments came when she accepted that she would no longer have Alvin and what he did, and how much she would miss his ability to distract her, but also make her feel as if she was alive, open to feeling intensely, whether good or bad. Without Alvin, the only one around to hurt her would be herself.

She was sorry about what had happened to Alvin, and knew she shared a sadness with other women. How many? Who knew? But as intense and as intimate as what they shared had been, she also understood that she did not know the man at all, aside from his hunger, aside from his need to meet her desire for domination.

Done with his stretching, John trotted down the hill to the roundabout. Breakfast was still being served, as many guests liked to sleep in, especially on Sunday. At the bell, John hit the timer on his digital watch—a habit he had developed after forgetting his watch that one time—the signal his run had officially begun. He darted down the exit road, focused on repeating the same rhythmic arm swing, in cadence with each leg driving forward and back. He looked towards the security shack to give Yankee the perfunctory wave, something that was as much a part of the routine as checking his watch. But Yankee wasn't in the shack. John saw him shimmying up a palm tree ladened with coconuts. John turned his attention back to the road, ready to exit the gate. But he noticed that waiting near the bottom of the tree, for Yankee to shake free some coconuts, maybe even open a few for drinking, was Yankee's wife Olive, the two younger boys, and the new baby in a worn looking pram.

John wanted to keep going. He was in total run mode and did not like to disturb the ritual and routine of this one moment he had to himself. But John had not yet seen the new baby, born almost three months ago. He had never properly congratulated Olive either.

He slowed down, trotted to the tree.

The two boys gathered coconuts off the ground to bring home while Yankee slid down the trunk. He and Olive both seemed surprised that John was there.

"Hello, sir," Yankee said.

"Morning. I was on my way out for my training, but I saw Olive and the baby here and realized that I've never extended proper congratulations. And I have a soft spot for babies and wanted to meet her. A girl, right?"

"Yes," Olive said. "A beautiful baby girl who we both love dearly."

"The name Ophelia," Yankee said. "After the muddah."

John circled around to the front of the pram. Ophelia slept peacefully, like an angel, a thin, pink headband fashioned into a bow crowned her head, elegant long eyelashes.

"She's absolutely beautiful," John whispered as he leaned over the pram. But he must have spoken too loudly, because Ophelia stirred. She opened her eyes. John stared. It was as if the air he breathed out had been suddenly sucked back in, like the way the water had flooded forward then receded back off the beach, shallow and dry, for a brief period after Hugo had moved on.

Ophelia had the beautiful black skin of her mother, but with the brightest blue eyes.

A choking sound from his throat was all John could manage as he straightened up abruptly. He looked at Olive, then Yankee, both with deep, dark brown eyes.

Alvin was the only local John had met on the island with those blue eyes.

Olive picked up the baby, held her close in her arms, walked towards the bay with the boys, but not before kissing Yankee on the cheek.

John wanted to move on, get his legs going, fast, sprint out the gate, down the road, past the almost completely buried airplane, all the way past Bolans before he even thought about turning around and coming back.

"You look thirsty, Mr. John," Yankee said. "Walk me to the shack."

Yankee picked up a large coconut, led the way. John stumbled after him.

At the shack, Yankee pulled his stool out onto the grass. He grabbed his machete from inside, placed the coconut on the ground in front of him, between his feet. He looked up at John.

John's hands shook. He still wanted to dash off, put this all behind him.

The two men studied each other.

"Sometimes," Yankee said, "a man needs to do the hardest things to hold on to true love."

Yankee raised the machete high in the air with his right arm, then drove it clean through the coconut, the sharpness of the blade cleaving the fruit into two perfect halves. With his left hand, he held up half of the coconut, splashing with milk, to John.

As he ran, John remembered that he had reached for the coconut half, drank from it, gave it back to Yankee, mumbled some sort of thank you, then took off. But his feet did not take him out towards the gate, up along the desolate road. Instead, he headed back towards the roundabout. He believed he sprinted. He made a right turn at the bell, straight up the bluff road to his house. He burst through the front door.

"Becca!"

His tone had the same urgent quality as on the morning he woke her to say the storm was coming.

"Everything okay?" she yelled, as she darted from her bedroom, down the stairs.

They met in the foyer. He threw his arms around her, squeezed as hard as he could without hurting her, kissed her deeply on the mouth, their tongues gently grazing. When they disengaged, they were both out of breath as they stared deeply into the other's eyes.

"I love you very much, Becca. I really do."

She kissed him again. Something about his tone was more heartfelt. She matched it. "And I love you very much."

John unstrapped the digital watch from his wrist, tossed it into the basket that rested on the small table.

"I'm not running anymore."

ACKNOWLEDGEMENTS

I want to thank my editor, Kristina Makansi, for her hard work, patience, and contributions to the final edits of this novel. It's great to work with someone who cares.

I want to thank my significant other, who read so many drafts and provided invaluable feedback. It can never be done without you. Most of all, thank you for opening my heart and inspiring the full bloom of the love and kindness we share.

Lastly, I want to thank the wonderful citizens of Antigua for all you taught me during so many joyous summers, for the musical lilt of your words, the cool rhythms of your calypso, the hearty warmth of your hospitality, the remarkable resiliency that stared down Hurricane Hugo and sent him on his way. Your island, with its soft sand, cool breezes, and tranquil waters, is a paradise I'll never forget.

ABOUT THE AUTHOR

SURVIVING THE STORM is I.J. Miller's eighth book, the seventh work of literary fiction. The novel, SEESAW, was translated into German and Spanish, and the Bantam paperback went through four printings while selling over 132,000 copies. WHIPPED was also translated into German and published by Penguin/Random House. The audio version of WUTHERING NIGHTS (Grand Central Publishing), was nominated for an Audie Award in 2014. Miller's short stories have appeared in numerous anthologies, including THE MAMMOTH BOOK OF BEST NEW EROTICA, Volumes 12 and 13. In 2022, Miller co-authored the memoir of a famous plastic surgeon entitled PROMISE FULFILLED, which is out in English and Spanish. Miller also earned an MFA as a Screenwriting Fellow at the American Film Institute. In 2020, the screenplay BAD DAY FOR THE DOG was a semi-finalist in the Unique Voices Screenwriting contest. Miller credits seventeen summers of working on the Caribbean islands of Antigua, St. Kitts, and St. Lucia with the inspiration for SURVIVING THE STORM.

Visit ijmiller.com.